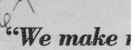

"We make

"Claims are two-edged swords, señorita. You may wish to renounce yours—and that is your right. But I have no intention of renouncing mine. And that is my right. And my duty."

Cathy understood the threat, felt it like a pain in her bones, tasted it on her tongue like the taste of fear. How could she have ever thought that Javier's eyes were warm? They were cold, cold as the deadliest Toledo steel.

DIANA HAMILTON is a true romantic at heart and fell in love with her husband at first sight. They still live in the fairy-tale English Tudor house where they raised their three children. Now the idyll is shared with eight rescued cats and a puppy. But despite an often chaotic life-style, ever since she learned to read and write, Diana has had her nose in a book—either reading or writing one—and plans to go on doing just that for a very long time to come.

Don't miss any of our special offers. Write to us at the following address for information on our newest releases.

Harlequin Reader Service
U.S.: 3010 Walden Ave., P.O. Box 1325, Buffalo, NY 14269
Canadian: P.O. Box 609, Fort Erie, Ont. L2A 5X3

DIANA HAMILTON

In Name Only

Harlequin Books

TORONTO • NEW YORK • LONDON
AMSTERDAM • PARIS • SYDNEY • HAMBURG
STOCKHOLM • ATHENS • TOKYO • MILAN
MADRID • WARSAW • BUDAPEST • AUCKLAND

ISBN 0-373-11896-1

IN NAME ONLY

First North American Publication 1997.

Copyright © 1994 by Diana Hamilton.

CHAPTER ONE

HE WAS tall for a Spaniard and he had grey eyes. A warm, smoky grey, intensified by lashes as thick and as black as his straight, soft hair. But the warmth, the softness, was quite definitely counterbalanced by the grave features, the heavy straight brows, by the unsmiling sensual line of his mouth.

She didn't know him, but she knew of him, Cathy thought on a flutter of panic as she fingered the square of white pasteboard he had handed her. Javier Campuzano.

And she knew why he had come, or thought she did, and she wanted to shut the door in his handsome, unsmiling face and pretend he was simply a bad dream. Or nightmare. Cathy shivered and the instinctive, convulsive tremor had more to do with his presence than with the unpleasant draught of cold air that sliced up from the drearily dank stairwell.

Behind her, in the tiny sitting-room of her modest north London flat, Johnny gave a cross between a crow and a squeal, carrying the undertones of impatience he always produced at the approach of a mealtime. She saw the Spaniard's eyes flicker, breaking the unfriendly, steady regard, and she stiffened her spine protectively, reminding herself that although she was in for an unenviable few minutes it would soon be over and the unsavoury Campuzano episode could be safely put behind them.

Unsavoury apart from the end-result, of course — her darling, precious Johnny. . .

'Señorita Soames?' He repeated his question, his

slightly accented, intriguingly sexy voice gathering the strength of steel, an impatience perhaps, engendered by the promise of a full-throated bellow from the hungry baby in the background. 'If you will permit. . .?'

A strong brown hand made a controlled but decisive gesture towards the interior of the flat, and Cathy pushed her paint-stained fingers through the blonde silk of her hair, thrusting it away from her face, and answered resignedly, 'Of course. Do come in, Señor Campuzano.' He wouldn't stay long, only as long as it took to tell her that no way would his impressive family lay themselves open to blackmail, emotional or otherwise. And she, *in loco parentis*, would take it, then show him the door.

She had expected the black-coated Jerezano, now head of one of Spain's most respected and wealthiest sherry families, to show a certain amount of unconcealed distaste for the poky room, cluttered with baby and oil-painting impedimenta, where not even her best efforts with wallpaper and soft furnishings could disguise what it was: an undesirably cramped conversion in a run-down area of the city.

But his eyes were on the baby, a slow, unreadable look which, unaccountably, made Cathy shudder all over again. At five months old, Johnny was a sturdy child, already with a definite character and opinions of his own. He saw few people—strangers had not yet entered his tiny world—and now he stopped jouncing his baby-bouncer over the cheap and cheerful carpet and, his starfish hands clutching the string of colourful beads fastened in front of him, he stared at the tall, dark interloper from deep grey, serious eyes. And if Javier Campuzano couldn't detect the obvious family likeness in the slightly olive-toned skin, those huge dark eyes, the mop of silky black hair, then he had to be blind.

But she didn't want him to see the likeness, did she? she reminded herself tersely. Just let him say his piece and leave, never to come near any of them again. And then Johnny smiled, showing two tiny, newly emerged front teeth, and it was like the sun coming out on a rainy day. And, amazingly, Campuzano smiled too — a smile of such sincerity that her breath was whisked away, leaving a vaccum, until the protective urge filled the gap and she scooped the baby from the bouncer, holding him on her slender hip, her violet eyes stormy with an ill-defined antagonism as she stared defiantly at the child's undoubted uncle, her soft mouth compressed.

'You've come on behalf of your brother Francisco,' she stated quickly, feeling a wayward pulse beat strongly, warningly, at the base of her throat as his smile vanished into glacial facial rigidity. But better to get this out of the way at once, get it all over and done with. 'I — we — ' she corrected herself automatically ' — lay no claim whatsoever on your family. Not now, nor in the future.' Not for the first time she wished Cordy had never sent that second letter. The complete silence following the first had been telling enough.

Francisco Campuzano, younger brother of the head of the distinguished family whose business empire stretched way beyond the world of vineyards, *bodegas* and wine shippers, had obviously ignored the fact that he had sired a son. The total silence that had followed that first letter, when Cordy had written to say she was pregnant, had clearly demonstrated that he preferred to forget that he had spent the night with a sexy English blonde who was on a modelling assignment in Seville.

So the head of the family's presence here now, at this late stage, could only indicate that he meant to put the damper on any ambitions the mother of the child might have regarding the Campuzanos' wealth and standing. And that was fine by her, she thought, smiling down at Johnny, who had decided to explore her mouth, pushing his tiny fingers against her even white teeth.

'Mam-Mam-Mam. . .'

Cathy's smile broadened and, just for a moment, she forgot the presence of the Spaniard. She was quite unashamed of assuring herself that the first coherent sounds the baby had produced, only a day or two ago, meant that he recognised her as his mother. And she was his mother, she thought staunchly, maybe not biologically, but in every other way that mattered. And soon, if the adoption went through smoothly, he would legally be hers. If she lived to be a thousand she would never be able to understand how Cordy could have abandoned him so callously.

But the quality of the silence had her uneasily raising her eyes to meet the steady grey regard of the Jerezano. And the unconsciously tender smile was wiped from her face as she registered the detailed assessment that ranged from the top of her blonde head down to her comfortable old canvas shoes, an assessment that suddenly, and inexplicably, made her aware of her body in a way she had never been aware before, a way that seemed to blister her skin.

'Yes, I recognise you,' Campuzano stated with a cool decisiveness that took Cathy's already ragged breath away and brought a puzzled frown to her smooth, wide brow. He took a step or two back, just avoiding the easel and canvas, as if to gain further perspective, the faint query in his smoky eyes—as if he doubted his own statement—melting away as he pronounced, 'At that party in Seville you wore the glamour of your trade. I stayed only moments—as a duty, you understand. You were one of the team who had been working on publicity brochures for my hotels. But I was there long enough to see you draped over Francisco.' For an infinitesimal moment his voice caught, then firmed, 'And after seeing the child for myself—won't you tell me his name?—I can only accept your claims.'

So he believed she was Cordy! Cathy thought with an inner quiver of incipient hysteria. Cordy would be furious if she ever discovered that anyone could possibly get the two of them mixed up! But caution silenced her instinctive denial, and she told him coolly, 'His name is John.'

She had learned caution or, rather, had it thrust upon her when, after the death of their mother, she had become more or less responsible for her younger sister. Even then, Cordy had been a handful, self-willed, vain and already showing signs of the unscrupulousness that would lead to the abandonment of her child. Cathy had been dismayed, but not surprised, when she had learned of the pregnancy.

'Juan.' Javier Campuzano used the Spanish pronunciation and Cathy bit back the objection she might have made as being unworthy and said instead, her voice distinctly edgy,

'You'll have to excuse us.' She hoisted the baby higher into her arms, cradling her cheek against the downy softness of his. Already he was beginning to look a bit square round the mouth. Any moment now he would show his displeasure at the lateness of his meal with bellows of rage which would rock the room. 'I have to mix his feed.' And one—she hoped—parting shot. 'I thought I'd made it clear. We make no claims.'

'We?' He was not to be so easily banished, she realised, watching the black bars of his straight brows draw together as his eyes flicked down to her ringless fingers. 'Who are "we"?'

'Johnny and I, of course,' she answered with a blitheness that was part bravado, part guilt. But Cordy had walked away from her baby, making it clear she didn't need the encumbrance, and that, in her book, meant that her selfish sister had automatically forfeited any rights to make claims of any kind.

'Ah.' Something that looked remarkably like relief flickered across those memorable features, then, 'But he is hardly old enough to make that sort of decision,' Campuzano remarked drily, the sensual mouth turning down at the corners, the arrogance in the way he held his head making her want to slap him. 'And you?' Broad shoulders shrugged beneath expensive black cashmere, ingrained courtesy softening the insult as he added, 'Are you prepared to convince me of some newly discovered sense of maturity and responsibility?'

Swallowing the impulse to tell him that he was mistaken, that she wasn't the woman who had been irresponsible enough to make love with a man she barely knew, unprotected against conception, who had been immature enough to go to bed with a man she had met for the first time a scant few hours before, Cathy was mortified to feel her face begin to flame. And he read the violent blush as an admission of something more serious than mere shortcomings — of course he did — and one black brow drifted upwards as he drawled, 'I think not.' He smiled, a humourless indenting of his lips, as if he was fully aware of how the sheer power of his presence robbed her of speech, of breath.

His personality was too strong, smooth and deadly, and his presence in this room seemed to electrify the very air she breathed. She had been right to be cautious, she comforted herself, clutching the now squirming baby closer, and just how right her instincts had been was brought violently home when he told her, the suavity of his sexy voice serving only to emphasise the underlying brutality, 'Claims are two-edged swords, *señorita*. You may wish to renounce yours — and that is your right. But I have no intention of renouncing mine. And that is my right. And my duty.'

She understood the threat, felt it like a pain in her bones, tasted it on her tongue like the taste of fear. How could she have ever thought his eyes were warm? They were cold, cold as the deadliest Toledo steel. But her chin came up, the warmth of the wriggling child in her arms giving her all the courage she needed to fling witheringly, 'Are you trying to tell me that after all this time Johnny's father has decided he wants to claim his son?' Her cheeks were growing hotter by the second, her voice shriller, and she didn't care. She had to make it clear that any claims the reluctant father made would not be tolerated. Not now, not at this delicate stage of the adoption proceedings. But she couldn't admit to that, of course, and so she resorted to sniping, 'After ignoring Johnny's existence for five months, and the fact of his conception for seven months before that, his belated attentions are not welcome now. Or needed. And why didn't he come himself?' Her eyes flashed purple fire. 'Too cowardly? Did he send you to do his dirty work?'

For a timeless moment he looked as if his body, his features, had been painfully hewn from a block of ice, and then he said, his lips barely moving, '*Francisco está muerto.*'

She needed no translation. Her face was ashen, the word 'dead' ringing hollowly inside her skull. In the depth of his emotion he had instinctively reverted to his own language and, for her part, she could have bitten her tongue out. And, when she could, she said quietly, 'I'm sorry. I didn't know.'

'How could you?' For a fragment of time violet eyes met smoky grey in an instant of sympathy and understanding and, inexplicably, Cathy felt bound to him, bonded with something that went deeper than compassion. And she knew precisely how mistaken she'd been in imagining anything of the sort when he told her, urbanity again sitting easily as a cloak on his wide shoulders, 'As Juan's mother, you have undoubted claim. But that doesn't minimise my own. As Francisco is no longer here to legally recognise his son, then I take it upon myself to do so in the name of the Campuzanos. He is of our family, of our blood. And besides——' his eyes narrowed, not above taunting '—he is my heir. And now——' his tone gentled as he held out strong brown hands '—he is getting grumpy! Fix his feed. I will hold him. And don't worry. . .' He smiled tightly into her apprehensive eyes. 'I won't spirit him away. Leave doors open to keep an eye on me, if you don't trust me.'

It was a challenge she had to accept, but how could she trust him when she didn't know what he wanted? To absorb Johnny into the Campuzano family? He'd made that much clear. But to what extent? Her hands shook as she got the water and mixed the formula, and her soft lips were compressed as she gave thanks for the instinct that had urged her to keep the truth from him.

If he knew that his nephew's mother had abandoned him. . . Cathy gritted her teeth; she couldn't bear to think about that.

'You take him, if you're so concerned. Adopt him, or something, with my blessing,' Cordy had said as soon as it had become obvious that Francisco Campuzano had no intention of acknowledging his son.

Cordy had seen the baby as a pawn, a key to unlock
the door that would lead to marriage into wealth and
prestige, and when that obviously wasn't going to
happen she didn't want to know.

As it was, the Jerezano believed she had the greater
claim to the baby, as his mother. And that was something he must go on believing—until the adoption
order had safely gone through, at the very least.

Squeals of delight were coming from the living-room
as she carried the bottle through, and her eyes widened
in disbelief. Javier Campuzano had discarded his coat,
the expensive, beautifully tailored garment flung haphazardly over the back of a chair, and he was bouncing
the crowing baby on his impeccably suited knees,
strong hands supporting the sturdy little body, his own
face lit with a smile that gave an entirely and heart-
stopping new dimension to his lean and handsome
features.

Relaxed, he was a man she could find irresistibly
attractive, she acknowledged dizzily as her heart began
to beat again, picking up speed as if to make up for
lost time. And that was something she hadn't admitted
in a long time, not since Donald.

But she recognised the momentary foolishness for
what it was as, becoming aware of her hovering presence, he rose elegantly to his feet, holding the baby
securely against his shoulder, the smile wiped away as
if it had never been as he told her, 'The preliminaries
are over, *señorita*. I now propose to lay my cards on
the table.'

Oh, did he? Cathy stamped on the impulse to tell
him to get lost, and took the baby without a word.
Settling herself on the chair she always used to nurse
Johnny, she told herself that it wouldn't hurt to hear
what he had to say. As long as he believed she was the

child's mother she didn't have to agree to a single thing.

He took his time over settling himself in the chair on the opposite side of the gas fire, and his eyes were coldly determined as he told her, 'Having seen you and recognised you, having seen Juan, I can't dispute that he is Francisco's son. One day I will show you photographs of my brother at roughly the same age. You would swear they were twins, if you didn't know better.'

Was she supposed to make some comment? She was too edgy even to look his way, and kept her eyes on the contentedly sucking baby. And Campuzano continued smoothly, 'I intend to make sure that Francisco's son is brought up in full knowledge of his Spanish heritage. One day he will inherit, become head of the family. Do you have the remotest idea of what that means?'

Forced by the edge of steel in his voice to emerge from the wall of uninterest she had carefully hidden herself behind, Cathy raised unwilling eyes and met the cold intensity of his. She shivered, forcing a cool disbelief into her voice as she queried, 'Have you no sons of your own to inherit, *señor*?' and saw his mouth compress to a line that was as bitter as it was brief, and, oddly, felt wildly exultant. Somehow she had flicked him on the raw, and surely it wasn't too ignoble of her to rejoice in the knowledge? Ever since he had announced himself she had been feeling apprehensive, edgy and very, very vulnerable, so paying him back felt good!

But her elation lasted no time at all because, as she eased the teat out of the baby's mouth and lifted the sleepy bundle against her shoulder, she saw Campuzano's eyes follow every gentle movement with an intentness that was infinitely disturbing and heard him say, 'My wife died. There were no children. I have no desire to replace her—much, I might add, to my mother's disapproval. However——' he spread his hands in a gesture that Cathy found poignantly fatalistic '—I looked to Francisco to marry and provide heirs. But he died.'

But left an heir. Battening down her agitation, Cathy got to her feet and carefully laid the child in his Moses basket, tucking the blankets around his body, the reward of a tiny, sleepy smile and the downdrift of thick black lashes making her loving heart twist in anguish.

Javier Campuzano would take him from her if he could; the dark intent, the threat, had been threaded through everything he had said so far.

She turned, finding him, inevitably, at her shoulder, his brooding eyes on the child. She wanted to scream, to make him go away and never come back, and, to hide her reaction, defuse a little of the pressure he was putting her under, she said quickly, 'I was sorry to hear of Francisco's death, but he can't have been much interested in his son's existence, otherwise he would have contacted my. . .' She caught herself just in time, and altered quickly, 'Answered one of my letters.'

Her face flushed. She wasn't used to dissembling. Her character was straightforward and direct, but she was fighting for Johnny, for the right to keep him, for the right to give him all the love his natural mother was incapable of feeling. And she didn't want all the unwilling sympathy he aroused when he told her with painful simplicity, 'About a week after your. . . encounter—shall we call it?—he was involved in a car accident which left him hooked up to a life-support system. He was in a coma for many months and when he regained partial consciousness he was paralysed. His eventual death must have come, for him at least, in the form of a release. When your letters arrived my mother's housekeeper put them aside. They were forgotten until I came across them two weeks ago when I began putting my brother's effects in order. Maria was not to blame. She was, like the rest of us, distraught by what had happened, by the fact that Francisco couldn't open his own mail, much less read it. I know, however, that he would have acknowledged his son.' He drew himself up to his full, intimidating height, deeply rooted family pride marking his features with a formidable severity.

Cathy's breath caught in her throat as she unwillingly admitted to his dark male magnificence, but she fought the grudging admiration as he added scathingly, 'If you'd got to know him at all, you too would know that much, at least. I can't know, of course, how deep the emotional side of your brief relationship went, but from your reaction to the news of his death I would judge it to have been regrettably shallow on your part.'

'Oh. . . I. . .' Cathy floundered. She had been forced into an unsavoury corner, and raked her memory for Cordy's explanation of events. Self-protectively, she dropped back into her chair, drawing her legs up beneath her. 'We had two glorious days and nights,' Cordy had confided. 'Eating, drinking, making love. Not much sleeping. From what he told me, and what I picked up from discreet enquiries, he comes from a fabulously wealthy family. Just one older brother who runs the whole family show—a bit of an enigma from what I can gather, but we can rule him out, because you know how the Spanish have this thing about pride and honour, and the importance of family? So, by my reckoning, I'm on to a winner! He was pretty cut up when I had to leave Seville, of course, and I did promise I'd let him know when I had some free time to entertain him in London. But you know how busy I've been.' She had given an elegant shrug. 'Never mind, I just know he'll be delighted when he gets the news. I'm going to write and tell him, get it down in black and white.'

Aware that Javier was waiting for some reply, Cathy frantically edited what she had learned of the brief affair from her sister and came up, lamely, with, 'We only knew each other for a couple of days.' She knew she sounded defensive, and that was down to the circumstances, the way she was having to go against her instincts and lie. And there wasn't anything she could do about that.

'Long enough, however, for your child to be conceived,' he replied with a dryness that shrivelled her bones. Slowly, his eyes never leaving her face, he drew two sheets of paper from an inside pocket and spread them out in front of her. 'Obviously, from reading your letters, up until five months ago you wanted Francisco to know of the existence of his child. You did write these letters of your own free will?'

What could she say? To deny it would let him know more than was safe. She nodded mutely, hating the web of deceit that was enmeshing her more firmly by the moment. And she felt even more guilty when he remarked, a thread of humour in his voice, 'You sign your name indecipherably. You are the mother of my nephew—I think I should know your name, don't you? Try as I might, I can't fathom it.'

She didn't blame him. The letters were written in Cordy's affected, flamboyant style, and were not too difficult to read, with patience. But the signature was something else: an enormous C connected to a Y which could have been any letter under the sun, with a mere squiggle in between. She cleared her throat and answered stoically, 'Cathy. Short for Catherine.'

'So, Cathy, what were you looking for? A financial settlement—or marriage?' His voice had hardened, making her heart beat faster. Besides, he had come closer, crowding her, swamping her with the power of his presence. 'Why the repudiation of all claims now?'

'Because I now realise that Johnny and I can make it on our own. We don't need any help; we make no claims—not one—especially now that Francisco is dead.' She spoke firmly simply because she was on firm ground. She was speaking the truth and was comfortable with that.

'I see.' He had begun to prowl the confines of the small room, like a supremely confident predator who was simply biding his time before making his kill. Cathy stuck her chin out. She wasn't going to let him frighten her. As long as he believed her to be Johnny's mother there was little he could do. Surely? 'And who takes care of the child while you are out posing for the camera?' he demanded to know. 'Some hired half-wit who doesn't care for his well-being or mental development so long as she gets paid at the end of the day? And do you have access to a garden where he can play safely when he is old enough? I saw no sign of one.' He picked up Cordy's letters, folded them carefully, and tucked them away in his pocket, his probing eyes never leaving hers.

That was a problem, she had to admit, but she'd get round it somehow.

'There are plenty of parks I can take him to,' she returned spiritedly. And so there were, and, if they weren't exactly on the doorstep, well, they'd manage. There were such things as buses, even in this part of London! 'And I look after him myself. I earn enough to keep us very adequately by my painting.' Not exactly true. Since leaving the agency she'd managed to get some freelance illustrating work occasionally and she'd sold a few oils through a small gallery in a not quite fashionable mews in the Kensington area. Money was often tight, but one day her name would be known and her work would be in demand. She just had to believe it.

'So?' He raised one straight brow, turning to the canvas on the easel. She always worked on a small canvas; it suited the restrained elegance of her style. And this one was of a little-known area of one of the oldest parts of London, very atmospheric and her first actual commission. But, whatever his thoughts on the merit of her work, they were kept firmly to himself, and when he turned to face her his expression was blank, but she caught the faint undertone of sarcasm as he commented, 'A woman of varied talents. But, if I am not mistaken, it can take many years for an artist to become known. And what happens in the meantime? You starve, or you return to your former, more lucrative career. Leaving Juan—where?'

He was insufferable! How dared he imply that she would fail in her care for the child? Violet eyes narrowed to stormy purple slits as she growled, 'I've had enough of this inquisition! I am perfectly capable of—'

'*Silencio!*' A flash of Spanish fire erupted deep in his eyes and he thrust his hands into the pockets of his superbly tailored trousers as if to prevent himself from strangling her on the spot.

His straddle-legged stance was intimidating enough, but his hard-bitten words were terrifying, making her stomach churn sickeningly as he informed her, 'Whether you like it or not, I intend to have a great deal of say in the way my nephew is brought up. I want him in Spain, with me. I want him at my home in Jerez where he will be given every advantage, every care, where he will learn how to shoulder the responsibilities of his inheritance, when the time comes. And don't think I come unarmed, *señorita*. I do not.'

He gave her a slow, terrible smile that turned her heart inside out with the awful knowledge that he meant every word he said. 'If you do not agree I will apply through your courts for a contact order. And I will get it; be sure of that. It will give me the right to take the child regularly to Spain, to bring him up as his father would have done. And I might go further,' he warned with icy control. 'With the help of the best lawyers available I could prove that you are not a fit mother.' His eyes derided her gasp of outrage. 'A second-rate model who gets drunk at parties and goes to bed with the first man she fancies. Don't forget, I saw you with Francisco. You could hardly stand. You were practically begging him to take you to bed; anyone with eyes could see that. There are countless witnesses I could call on to vouch for it, and I am quite sure—' again that terrible mocking smile '—that, should I wish to delve into your former career, I could find many more instances of your promiscuity. Added to which, your sudden and vague idea of supporting yourself and your son by selling paintings smacks a little of instability, wouldn't you say? And who is to predict when single-parenthood will begin to bore you? How long before you pine for the glamour, the spurious attention, the parties? Not long, I think. However—' he reached for his coat, barely glancing at Cathy's pale, anguished face '—I might be persuaded not to go so far. If you agree to accompany me and Juan to Spain—unfortunately, at his tender age, you will have to be part of the package—to meet his grandmother for a protracted visit, then I will not take the matter any further. But I do warn you that if you refuse I will then put the other matters in hand.'

He gave her a thin smile, one that boded no good at all.

'Adiós, señorita. I will call tomorrow at the same

time to hear what you have decided. And then the arrangements can be put in hand. Either way. And think very carefully. If you try to go against me, you will lose him. This I promise.'

CHAPTER TWO

'PERHAPS the warmth of the Andalusian sun will unfreeze your vocal cords,' Campuzano tendered with a derisory narrowing of smoky grey eyes.

Stepping out of the small airport building ahead of him, Cathy had to admit that his remark was justified. Her thoughts had been too clamorous, too spiced with anxiety, to allow her to do more than offer monosyllabic mutters in return for his conversational overtures, until he had given up, relaxing into his club-class seat, apparently falling asleep with total ease.

His ability to switch off completely was something she envied. She had spent the entire two and a half hours of the flight in an excess of agitation, misgivings and self-recrimination. Thankfully, the baby had slept in her arms since take-off at Gatwick, but he was now beginning to stir. She lifted him gently against her shoulder and Campuzano offered, 'Let me take him. He is heavy.'

'No.'

Unconsciously Cathy's arms tightened around the small body, every fibre of her being on the defensive, and Campuzano said softly, his dark voice a confident near-whisper, 'As you like. But I wouldn't put money on how soon you will gladly hand over the burden of his care. I never bet on certainties.'

A remark which was almost totally justified by the lies she had allowed him to believe, she thought sickly, although it hardly excused his lack of basic politeness, and she closed her eyes briefly against the glare of the midday sun, the deep and improbable blue of the sky.

24

Spring in England this year had been unusually cold
and wet, and the intense warmth of the Spanish sun,
even in early May, sent a reactionary shudder through
her, not relaxing her one little bit. And Campuzano
said, his voice aloof now, 'You are tired. Tomás should
be here with the car at any moment.' And, as if his
words had the instant power of command, a large black
Mercedes drew up in front of them and, at the flick of
imperious fingers, the airport official who had rushed
to take charge of the luggage — mostly Johnny's —
pushed the trolley forward with a self-important bustle.

How arrogant he was, she thought wearily. A flick
of his fingers was enough to have everyone around
rushing to please. He was used to getting exactly what
he wanted, when he wanted it, and if the occasion ever
arose when he didn't get instant gratification his initial
reaction would be, she guessed, total amazement.
Followed by swift and terrifying anger.

Well, she was about to amaze him, wasn't she? He
wanted Johnny — or Juan, as he insisted on calling him.
He wanted, and intended to get, total control where
his nephew was concerned. And that he would never
have, she vowed staunchly.

Ever since Cordy had made it plain that she had no
time for the child, she, Cathy, had taken the good-as-
motherless scrap straight to her heart. She had done
everything for him, and gladly, even giving up her job
as an illustrator with the advertising agency she'd
worked at since leaving college so that she could be
with the baby day and night. So no, this time Javier
Campuzano was not going to have things all his own
way.

That she had had no option, in the circumstances,
other than to fall in with his commands that she bring
the child to Jerez was something she wasn't going to
think too deeply about. She preferred to look on the

few weeks she had agreed to spend here as an opportunity to demonstrate just what a caring, responsible mother she was. Javier Campuzano would probably remain stubbornly blinkered in that respect, but surely she would find an ally in the baby's grandmother? A mother herself, she would understand that Johnny's place was with her, in England, that devoted maternal love weighed more heavily than all the material advantages of the Campuzano dynasty.

The airport official and the swarthy, stockily built uniformed chauffeur, Tomás, had finished stowing the luggage in the boot of the car and now held the rear door open. Cathy, her heart down in her shoes, stepped unwillingly forward. Every day since the Jerezano had appeared on her doorstep had seen the steady, inexorable erosion of her desired position, and getting into this car now seemed to signify the closing of the door to her past hopes and intentions.

Sliding into the air-conditioned coolness, Cathy told herself not to be a fool and settled the baby more comfortably on her lap. Somehow she would find a way out of the mess she was in. Then she flinched as Campuzano got in beside her. Automatically her body tensed. He was too close, overpoweringly so. She caught the downward drift of his smoky eyes, the scornful, mocking curl of his sensual mouth, and knew he had registered her reaction. And she told herself that the way she tensed up whenever he was near had everything to do with the threat he posed to her rights over Johnny and nothing whatsoever to do with all that unforced masculine magnetism.

Very aware of the powerful male thigh so close to her own, and knowing that he would undoubtedly construe further silence on her part as immature sulkiness, she asked stiltedly, 'Are we far from Jerez?'

It would soon be time for Johnny's feed, and he

needed changing, and Campuzano noted the tiny
anxious frown between her violet eyes and answered
drily as the car moved smoothly away from the airport,
'A mere seven kilometres. And it is pronounced
Hereth. However, you must wait in patience to enjoy
the luxuries of my town house. We shall be staying at
the *finca* for the first few days.'

'And how far is that, whatever it is?' She spoke more
snappishly than was wise, aggrieved because he had
automatically assumed that her anxiety to reach their
destination sprang from her desire to sample the life-
style of the rich and powerful. Was that how he had
viewed her complete capitulation a mere twenty-four
hours after he had delivered his initial ultimatum?

'"It" is the land, the vineyard, the house. And there
we shall stay, for the time being.' His haughty
expression did nothing to disguise his implacable will.
'And it is roughly nine kilometres from the airport in
the opposite direction from Jerez.' His voice dropped,
very silky, very smooth. 'But since you have assured
me that you no longer crave a hectic social life, the
isolation shouldn't trouble you.'

Had she been who she had said she was—Cordelia
Soames, model, sybarite and scalp-hunter—then the
isolation would have bothered her to the point of
screaming. As she was merely sister Cathy, two years
older in years but aeons younger in experience, it
didn't bother her a scrap, and what she had to do was
convince his high-and-mightiness that she, in her role
as Cordy, had completely changed.

Johnny was growing fractious, fists and feet punching
the air, and Cathy said sweetly, 'You can hold him
now,' and passed him over, earning herself a glance of
pleased surprise, then turned to look out of the
window, hiding her own wicked smile, because Señor
Javier Campuzano was just about to discover how

difficult it was to keep control of a strong, eighteen-pound baby who was determined to wriggle, not to mention the havoc a leaking nappy could wreak on a pair of expensively trousered knees!

'I am looking forward to meeting your mother,' she pronounced with the truth born of hope, injecting a liberal sweetness as she added, 'Is her English as good as yours?' She kept her gaze on the sun-drenched, rolling low hills which rose above the widely sweeping coastal plain, but, puzzled, her eyes were drawn back to him, unprepared for the rich vein of amusement in his voice.

'Almost. But the pleasure will have to be postponed for a while. She rarely visits the *finca*, preferring the house in Jerez.'

And that wiped the smile from her face. The sooner she made contact with Johnny's grandmother, the sooner she would find an ally to stand at her side against the man who was, moment by moment, reinforcing his position as her enemy. And what was almost as disappointing was the way he positively seemed to enjoy handling the lively baby, not one scrap put out by the way the tiny fists were creating havoc in the soft darkness of his expensively styled hair or by the ominous damp patches on those immaculately trousered knees!

Damn him! she muttered inside her head. Why couldn't he have left well alone? She and Johnny had been doing just fine until he had poked his arrogant nose into their affairs. The adoption would have eventually gone through, she just knew it would, despite the warning Molly had given her.

Molly Armstrong had been appointed guardian *ad litem* — a large and ponderous title for such a tiny, bubbly lady, Cathy had always thought — and, out of the many visits she'd made to compile her reports before the courts could consider the granting of an adoption order, a warm and friendly relationship had been born. And it had been Molly she'd phoned in a panic after Campuzano had left that first evening, and Molly, bless her, had made time for her in her busy schedule, appearing on the doorstep at nine the following morning, just as she'd finished giving the baby his bath.

'You've got problems?' Molly had said, taking the sturdy, towel-wrapped baby on her knee while Cathy had disappeared into the kitchen to make coffee. 'So tell me about them. Slowly. Don't gabble as you did down the phone last night.'

So over their drinks Cathy had told her, guiltily missing out the fact that she had lied, had allowed Javier Campuzano to believe she was Johnny's mother. She didn't feel easy about what she had done, but that erroneous belief had to strengthen her case where he was concerned. If he ever discovered that Johnny's real mother had walked out on him he would leave nothing undone — not a single thing — until he had legal and total control over his nephew.

'You and Señor Campuzano are both related to Johnny in the same degree,' Molly said, her neat head tipped on one side. 'Naturally, he could apply for an order to give him the right to see the child regularly, to exercise some control over his future upbringing and welfare.'

Which was precisely what Campuzano had said, but Cathy knew, she just knew, he wanted complete and total control. And she had no doubt at all that he would move heaven and earth to get it if he ever discovered that Johnny's real mother had walked out, preferring the glamour and excitement of a modelling career to the hard work of bringing up a child. So, 'And if the baby were still with his real mother?' Cathy asked, hoping she didn't look as hot and guilty as she felt. 'Would his father's family still have rights?'

'Well, I have warned you,' Molly answered, her smile sympathetic, 'that the adoption order might not go through, despite the natural mother saying she wanted nothing more to do with the child. The courts could take the view that, following the birth, she is suffering some kind of hormonal imbalance and could change her mind at a later stage. Only time will tell, of course, and, in the interim, you could be given a residence order with parental responsibility.' She was taking the question at face value, in view of the warnings she'd already given, and that made Cathy feel more devious than ever, her long hair falling forward, hiding her uncomfortable face as she dressed the baby. And Molly was telling her, 'And yes, the father's family would still have rights; a child needs the care and love of all its family.' Which was not at all what Cathy had wanted to hear.

And because of that she had had to back down, to agree to come to Spain. All she had to do now was convince the not-to-be-convinced that she was a responsible, loving mother.

She was in her own thoughts. Her mouth took a grim line and, made aware that he was looking at her, saying something, she shrugged half-heartedly. 'Sorry?'

'We are almost there. You can see the house from here.' The emphatic patience of his tone told her he was repeating himself. And then, with an edge of steel, 'I would have thought you would be eager to see where your child will be spending most of his boyhood.'

Unforgivable. Untrue. He was trying to make her believe that Johnny's future was already settled. She refused to dignify his taunt by making any comment. Casting a dismissive glance at the low white building perched on top of a rounded hill overlooking the vineyards, the rows of newly leafing vines curving around the hillsides in perfect symmetry, Cathy hunched one shoulder in a negligent shrug. She utterly refused to be impressed.

Johnny didn't need vineyards, or anything else Campuzano could give him. He needed love, and cherishing, and she could give him that in abundance. Unfortunately, the Spaniard seemed to be offering just that. The sternly arrogant features were relaxed, irradiated with intensely tender pleasure as he bounced the squealing baby on his knee.

Jealousy, white and piercing and utterly unpleasant, darkened her eyes, and her voice was thin and sharp as she instinctively reached for the child.

'Do you *want* to make him sick?' she asked, and was immediately, humiliatingly ashamed of herself, hardly able to contain her relief when the Mercedes swept through a wide arch in a long white wall and came to a well-bred halt in a courtyard that billowed with scarlet geraniums in huge terracotta pots.

However, for all her shame, she refused to hand Johnny over as Campuzano held the car door open, managing with unsteady defiance to lever herself to her feet, feeling the heat of the sun-baked cobbles burn through the soles of her sensible low-heeled shoes.

Seen at close quarters, the house was impressive: low and sprawling with thick, white-painted walls and a sturdy double-storey square tower at one end. The arcaded front elevation seemed to offer a cool refuge from the sun, with the harsh contrasts of the white walls, the deep blue of the sky, the vibrant, living colour of the purple bougainvillaea, all those spice-scented scarlet geraniums.

Cathy closed her eyes on a wave of homesickness, overpowered as much by the personality, the lithe strength, the sheer untamed grace of the Spaniard as by the almost bludgeoning vitality of his native Andalusia.

Transplanted from the soft greens and greys and blues of a reluctant English spring, she felt suddenly that the enormity of having to do battle with Javier Campuzano on his own territory was beyond her.

But, despite her quiet temperament, she was a fighter, she reminded herself. She would not simply give in, as the Spaniard was so obviously convinced she would. Straightening her drooping shoulders, she produced a hopefully imperious tone.

'Show me where I can feed and change the baby. He needs to be out of this sun.' Out of her need to hold her own she had managed to make it sound as though the vibrant energy of the Andalusian heat were in some obscure way obscene, and the eyes that challenged him were glinting with a purple spark of defiance.

'Of course.' He was clearly unimpressed by her attitude, and the lowering black bar of his brows put an edge on the courtesy of his smooth reply. He said something rapid in Spanish to Tomás, who was already extracting the luggage from the car. And the hand that gripped her elbow, steering her over the cobbles, wasn't gentle at all and she tugged distractedly away, shocked by the electrifying sensation produced by the hard pads of his lean fingers against her skin.

'Ahhh! El niño!'

A short, amazingly stout woman emerged from the arcaded shadows at a trot, black-clad arms extended, her wrinkled face wreathed with smiles, her attention all for the wide-eyed Johnny, the merest dip of her still glossy dark head for Cathy herself.

Admiring baby-talk had a universal language all of its own, Cathy learned as Johnny's chubby solemn face quickly dissolved in a smile of heart-wrenching brilliance, little arms held out to the newest member of his fan club. And before Cathy could catch her breath the baby was expertly whisked out of her arms and was carried away, chortling perfidiously, into the cool shade of the house.

'He will be perfectly safe,' Campuzano said with a taunting smile that set her teeth on edge. 'I'm sorry Paquita didn't stay long enough to be introduced, but you must excuse her lapse of manners—the Spaniard's love of children is legendary.'

'And that makes it all right, does it?' Cathy sniped. How could she get through to him, make him understand that she wouldn't be taken over, and, more importantly, wouldn't allow her baby to be, either?

He had moved infinitesimally closer and the harsh light of the sun illuminated the grainy texture of his tanned skin, the darker shadowing of his hard jawline, the golden tips of the black fan of the lashes that lowered in an unsuccessful attempt to hide the gleam of satisfaction in the smoky depths of his eyes.

Cathy's breath caught in her throat, an unborn sob, half frustration, half something else entirely—something she couldn't put a name to—choking her. And she looked away quickly, her soft lips drawn back against her teeth as she reiterated edgily, 'I told you— he needs to be fed and changed. He's not a plaything; he's——'

'I know precisely what he is.' His voice was a lash of rebuke. 'He is my nephew. And Paquita knows exactly what she's doing. She and Tomás, besides keeping house for me here, have brought up nine children of their own to lusty maturity.'

'Bully for them!' Cathy snapped with a cold curl of her lips. She knew what he was up to. She was to be relegated to the status of a spare wheel, a punctured one at that. The taking-over of the child had begun and all Campuzano had to do was wait until she grew bored enough to take herself off, back to her former glitzy career — or so he thought.

And her heated suppositions were proved entirely correct when he extended a slight smile — one that didn't touch his beautiful, cynical eyes — and offered, 'I will show you to your room. We dine at nine — I'm sure you can occupy yourself somehow until then.'

He moved towards the house, the effortless, almost unbelievable male arrogance and grace of his easy, long-legged stride making her hate him. Anger took her by the throat and her eyes were smouldering with resentment as she caught up with him, demanding, 'You can show me where that — that woman has taken my child. Looking after him will keep me occupied.' She wasn't about to be pushed into the background of Johnny's life. That wasn't the reason she had agreed to come to Spain, and the sooner he understood that, the better.

But he looked at her coldly, the ice in his eyes taking her breath away as he warned harshly, 'Be careful, señorita. I don't like your attitude any more than I like your morals. Paquita's position in my household demands respect. See that she gets it, and mind your manners. Come.'

Bristling with temper, Cathy followed stiff-leggedly into the house. She was aware of space and airiness, of white walls and cool, tiled floors, but of nothing much else until he paused before a plain cedarwood door, gave her a cursory dip of his handsome head, and said smoothly, 'Your room. Rosa, Paquita's youngest daughter, will come for you at nine to show you to the dining-room. I suggest you relax and try to mend your temper.'

He turned on his heels and was gone, leaving the memory of a definitely feral smile, leaving her even more incensed at his high-handed treatment of her.

Pushing the door open, her lips tight, she scowled into the silent, beautiful room, noted that the cases she had brought from England were stacked at the foot of a handsomely carved fruitwood bed, and closed the door again, leaning against it briefly as she glanced up and down the long corridor.

Every last one of the million and one things that a baby needed were packed in those cases. Which meant that Paquita couldn't be attending to his now urgent needs but probably tossing him like a cuddly football around her own multitudinous offspring, displaying the newest member of the oh, so dominant Campuzano family to an admiring audience. But admiration didn't satisfy hunger pangs or change wet nappies!

Determined to rescue him if it was the last thing she did, Cathy set off down the corridor, her chin at a pugnacious angle, opening each and every door. The arrogant Spaniard was going to have to learn that he couldn't, as of divine right, have everything his own way.

The three other bedrooms she glanced into were as beautiful and as silent as her own and, after the corridor angled, she found the communal living-rooms, places to eat, relax. And one study full of highly technical data and communications systems.

And then the kitchen, which must be the ground floor of the two-storey tower, because a curved wooden staircase led up from among the quietly humming electrical equipment which gleamed against the white-washed stone walls. She spared a reluctant thought for the nice mix of ancient and modern, the great stone chimney breast, the terracotta-tiled floors and lovingly polished carved dressers, before her eyes narrowed to glinting purple slits as she heard the unmistakable sound of crooning Spanish baby-talk coming from the room above.

So! She had tracked Johnny down, as she had known she eventually would. And this was where Paquita learned that she couldn't snatch the baby out of her arms and carry him off to play with him without so much as a 'May I?' while Campuzano stood by, gloating, that look of satisfaction on his hard, impossibly arrogant features!

Anger, fuelled by the fiercely protective mothering instinct that had hit her the moment it had become clear that Cordy regarded the new-born baby as little more than a pawn in the game she'd been playing, drove her up the stairs like a miniature whirlwind. But her rapid pace faltered almost as soon as she'd gained the upper room. Fitted out as a nursery, it contained everything a baby could need, and there was even a single bed alongside the capacious, comfortable crib. And far from being tossed around like a human football, Johnny was safely tucked into the arms of an exceedingly pretty girl of around eighteen years of age, a blissful expression on his chubby face as he sucked his bottle.

He had been changed and was wearing a romper she had never seen before, the all-in-one garment a soft blue cotton that had to be more suitable for this climate than anything she had brought with her. And the tiny fingers of one plump hand were entwined in the soft dark curls of the girl who was nursing him, she noted with a wrench. Johnny always played dreamily with her own long blonde locks as she fed him, part of the bonding process.

'Mama comes!' The hugely stout Paquita was hovering, her face wreathed in smiles, her rich voice soothing as she met Cathy's hurt, bewildered eyes. '*Mi hija—Rosa, mi hija. Inglés* not so good. Rosa good. All children *educado! Muy bueno*!'

'Mama is proud that all her children speak some

English. Some better than others.' Rosa's tone was gentle but her smile was brilliant, her voice attractively accented as she turned her attention to Cathy. 'Baby Juan has had his oatmeal; that is right, yes? And when Don Javier telephoned his instructions for what would be needed he told us the brand of the milk formula you used.' The teat was eased from the little drowsy mouth and Rosa expertly lifted the sleepy baby on to her shoulder.

'Let me.' Cathy stepped forward, taking the child, her loving arms enfolding him. She had no doubt that Javier Campuzano had planned every last tiny detail. Those cool eyes had missed nothing on his many visits to her London flat before they had left for Spain, while his clever brain had already determined that legal custody of his nephew was already as good as his—whether the means of obtaining it were fair or foul.

Cathy shivered as a deep, instinctive fear put ice in her veins, and Rosa got up from the nursing chair, gathering the empty bottle, the oatmeal bowl, asking, 'You are pleased with the nursery? I shall sleep here with him. I will look after him well, I promise.'

None of this was Rosa's fault, so Cathy swallowed the impulse to snap, The hell you will! and took her time over tucking the baby in his crib.

Her first instinctive impulse had been to demand that everything in the nursery be transported to her bedroom. Right now! But this room was ideal; the long windows set in the thick stone walls admitted sunlight and fresh air, and their louvred shutters could be closed during the heat of the day. It was handy for the kitchen, too, where she could make up his formula, store the day's supply of bottles in the fridge, mix his oatmeal and purée his vegetables. It would be neither sensible nor practical to insist on such a move. So, straightening, casting the baby a fond, lingering glance, she turned to Rosa.

'I will be looking after Johnny myself. He can take his daytime rests in here, but I shall have him in my room at night. We can carry the crib through after his evening bath and feed.' Then, seeing the utter desolation chase surprise out of the dark Spanish eyes, Cathy made the only compromise she was willing to consider. 'If I need to be out for any reason I'll be happy to leave him in your care.' Which didn't do much to lessen the look of hurt disappointment, and made her add, 'He should sleep for at least two hours now, but I'd be grateful if you'd keep an eye on him while I unpack.'

That she would need to leave the baby in Rosa's obviously capable hands some time in the near future was in no doubt, Cathy told herself as she stowed her belongings away in the capacious cupboards and drawers. If Johnny's grandmother didn't show up at the *finca* within the next few days, then she would have to go to Jerez and find her. Campuzano would have to learn that she couldn't be kept here in isolation, a virtual prisoner, separated for most of the time from the child they were tacitly fighting over.

Carrying the crib down to her room later that evening restored Cathy's confidence in her ability to hold her own with the overwhelming Jerezano. Rosa helped, and as they positioned the crib at the side of the big carved bed the Spanish girl said, 'Don Javier asked me to show you to the dining-room.' She consulted her watch. 'In one hour's time. And while you eat I will look in on the baby now and then.'

'I found the dining-room when I was looking for the nursery,' Cathy returned with a grin, placing the now sleeping child in the crib and covering him with a soft woollen blanket. 'But I'll be easier if you check on him, thanks.' She had taken to the Spanish girl on sight and Johnny responded to her well; the three of them had spent a happy hour and a half, enjoying bath-time, feed-time and playtime, with Paquita puffing up the stairs to join in the fun. So if Johnny woke while she was closeted in the dining-room with Campuzano he would be reassured by a familiar face.

Not that she was looking forward to dining with Johnny's uncle, of course. The odd, fluttery sensation deep inside her was due to apprehension about the way he would receive the ground rules she was determined to lay down, she assured herself as she stepped out of the shower in the cool green marble *en-suite* bathroom. He could turn awkward, she acknowledged. A strand of cruelty was woven into his proud Andalusian character, she just knew it. He would not be an easy man to cross.

Suppressing the inching, quivering feeling of alarm, Cathy dressed quickly in the simple, sleeveless black crêpe shift she had already laid out, and braided her long blonde hair. The minimum of make-up and she was ready, ten minutes early. A pity, that. Counting off the seconds to the coming confrontation could only put her already jangling nerves even more on edge.

Meeting her wide violet eyes in the mirror, she made a conscious effort to ease away the tiny frown line between her arching brows, and wondered again how Javier Campuzano could have mistaken her for Cordy.

At five feet seven, they shared the same height, and both had fine, clear skin and blonde hair to shoulder-blade length. But there, as far as Cathy was concerned, the resemblance ended. Cordy's blue eyes were more sapphire than violet, her cheekbones far more pronounced, her nose longer and slightly aquiline, giving her features far more sophistication than Cathy's. And whereas Cordy's figure was model-girl-svelte, truly

elegant, Cathy's curves were far more generous—
positively earthy, she sometimes felt.

But then he would no doubt put the weight gain
down to recent motherhood, and he had admitted he'd
only stayed at the party for a very short time. And she
hadn't put him right, had she?

She wasn't at all easy about the deception; in fact if
she thought about it for too long she ended up feeling
definitely ill! But she'd had no option and would keep
up the pretence to the bitter end, because if he ever
found out that she was merely Johnny's aunt, that his
real mother had done a bunk, then he would take
control of the baby and make sure there was nothing
she could do about it.

But it wouldn't come to that. She would lie until she
was blue in the face if she had to. And on that
positive—if reprehensible—thought she stiffened her
spine and strode forth to do battle with the man who
was her enemy.

CHAPTER THREE

'AN APERITIF, Cathy?'

She hovered in the open doorway and watched as he laid the papers he'd been engrossed in aside, his urbane smile not quite reaching his eyes as he rose to his feet.

'Thank you.' She sound breathless. Her heart was performing a mad tattoo against her breastbone. He rarely used her given name, preferring the formal '*señorita*', investing it with the delicate sarcasm she had come to dread. And now his lightly hooded eyes were making a lazy yet thorough inspection of her black-clad body and she saw his wide shoulders rise in a minimal shrug that barely moved the surface of the fine white alpaca jacket he wore.

Cathy turned on teetering heels, trying not to stumble as she made for one of the soft leather-covered armchairs arranged around the massive open fireplace, the chimney breast soaring way up to the raftered ceiling. The drift of his cool eyes had been a slow sexual insult, making her shatteringly aware of all that dominant Spanish machismo so tenuously concealed beneath the suave veneer of grace and good manners.

Warily, she watched as he poured the pale golden liquid from a bottle bearing the distinctive Campuzano label, and he sounded as if he were purring as he placed the curved, slender glass beside a silver bowl of plump olives on the low table at her side.

'Try the *fino*. If it is too dry for your palate we can substitute an *oloroso*. The British used to be our biggest market for the sweeter, heavier sherries — the drink for elderly maiden ladies, we consider it here —

41

but now their tastes appear to have changed; we now export far more *fino* to your country——'

'Don't knock it!' Cathy advised in a cold little voice. 'Maybe all those elderly ladies have acquired more sophisticated tastes. Or drink gin.'

Did he have to act so superior all the time? Or couldn't he help it because it was an integral part of his nature? The latter, she suspected, and was thrown off balance when he smiled—really smiled this time—as he assured her,

'I don't knock it, believe me. When Drake singed the beard of the King of Spain he also carried home around three thousand casks of sherry and so founded our highly profitable trade links with England. So no, I wouldn't dream of knocking one of our best markets!' He seated himself almost directly opposite her with an indolent grace that only served to remind her of his powerful masculine virility, his grey eyes appearing almost seductively drowsy as he questioned, 'Is the drink to your taste?'

Pulling herself away from the mesmeric spell of his hooded gaze, Cathy took a hasty sip and then another. The pale wine was crisp and delicious, slightly aromatic, the chilled liquid sliding down her throat, tasting like sunlight gently touched by frost.

'Very much so.' Her eyes smiled into his, her heart warmed by this rare moment of something she could almost believe to be closeness. 'I confess, I could become addicted.' Idly she traced a line in the condensation on the curved surface of the glass and heard herself asking with an interest she had never expected to feel, 'If the market for the sweet sherries is declining, why don't you produce more dry?'

'It is not so simple. It all depends on the development of the *flor*. . . However——' he spread his strong, finely made hands at her look of incomprehension and rose to refill her glass '—when we visit Jerez I will take you to the *bodega* where I shall attempt to explain. If you are interested.'

She was, almost in spite of herself, in spite of those feelings of mutual mistrust which flowed so strongly between them, the deceit on her part and the dictatorial arrogance on his. But he had given her an opening she couldn't pass and, taking another fortifying sip, she leant back in her chair, making an effort to relax, crossed her legs above the knee, and asked, 'When, exactly, shall I get to visit Jerez and your mother?'

'Why the hurry?' There was a touch of contempt in the steady grey gaze, a flick of something that made her shudder as his eyes deliberately assessed the long, exposed elegance of her crossed legs. 'Is the *finca* too quiet, too rustic for your tastes? *Lo siento*—I'm sorry you have become so quickly bored.'

Horrible, horrible man! Cathy's face turned an uncomfortable red as she hastily set her feet side by side and tugged down her skirt. He'd been looking at her unthinkingly exposed legs as if they were goods on offer—shoddy, second-hand goods—and instantly rejected them. Cordy—or her reputation—had a lot to answer for!

'My main reason for agreeing to come to Spain was to allow your mother to see her grandson,' she told him with a cool dignity she was proud of. 'If you won't take us to her, then I must find some means of going on my own. I'm sure Tomás——'

'My mother will receive you when she is ready,' he injected suavely. 'It is not so long since Francisco's death; she needs time to adjust to the idea that he left a child. And Tomás will take you nowhere; I forbid it.'

Forbid? Yes, he was perfectly capable of doing so. As far as he was concerned, his word was law and Tomás and every other subject in his kingdom would obey it right down to the very last letter. Something sharp and hot rose in her throat to choke her and her voice was hoarse with anger as she flung at him, 'Then what the hell am I doing here? Couldn't you have waited until she was ready to see him? Why waste my time?'

Anger turned back on her in waves of frustration as it met the unbreachable wall of his apparent disregard. There was not a flicker of emotion on those dark, impressive features, merely the schooled control of a man who had witnessed the demeaning antics of a fishwife but was too polite to comment. And she sagged back in her seat, suddenly drained, as he rose with inherent grace and pressed a discreetly concealed button near the wide cedarwood door.

'Come, it is time to eat.'

Just like that. Just as if her angry questions had never been asked, Cathy fumed, rising in a jerky movement, following him, wanting to get the meal over and done with and get back to her room, shut herself in with the sleeping baby, and try to work out what to do.

Facing him across the oval table, Cathy spread her linen napkin over her lap with a fierce twist of her wrist and waited for Paquita to serve her with, as she proudly announced, '*Sopa de mariscos al vino de Jerez*,' which, for her benefit, Campuzano translated more prosaically as sherry and shellfish soup.

Whatever, it was delicious and welcome. Cathy ate quickly and appreciatively, fully aware that she wouldn't have agreed to share his table at all if she hadn't been ravenously hungry.

The warm crusty bread served with the tangy, ocean-flavoured soup was irresistible, and Cathy, her mouth full, saw the lean brown hand slide a glass over the linen cloth, found her eyes held by the dusting of dark

hair between the white of his cuff and the soft leather
strap of his wafer-thin watch, and felt her throat close
up for no reason at all.

'*Manzanilla* makes the perfect accompaniment. Part
of the pleasure of savouring a meal,' he said softly,
coolly, and she replaced the spoon in her bowl and
swallowed her mouthful with immense difficulty. He
was letting her know that her table manners were no
better than a greedy child's. He never lost an opportunity to put her down. Her appetite disappeared very
suddenly.

'This comes from the Campuzano vineyards in the
area of Sanlúcar de Barrameda. It is believed that the
breeze from the Atlantic gives it its unique and slightly
salty flavour.' He took a reflective sip from his own
glass, his lightly veiled eyes challenging her fulminating
violet stare and, more as a reflex action than anything
else, she took an apprehensive sip. Salty sherry?

But it was crisp and cold and intriguingly tangy, paler
in colour than the chilled *fino* he had given her as an
aperitif, and if he noted the surprise, followed by the
pleasure in her eyes, he made no comment other than,
'Finish your soup. Paquita will be devastated if you
don't clear your plate.'

'I am not a child,' Cathy returned stiffly.

She felt his eyes slide over the lush curves of her
breasts, heard him agree, 'Obviously not,' and decided
to maintain a dignified silence, and managed to do
exactly that, right through the *Sevillana* salad, the
chicken with garlic and one glass too many of a light
Rioja wine.

'You will take a little caramel flan?' Paquita had
withdrawn, and the silver cake knife was poised in
long, lean fingers. Cathy shook her head. She couldn't
eat another crumb, and the wine, on top of all that

sherry, had gone straight to her head. She wasn't used to alcohol in such profligate quantity.

The silver serving knife was gently placed back on the linen-covered table and Campuzano leaned elegantly back in his chair, his attractively accented voice much too smooth as he remarked, 'I hear you have made Rosa redundant.' A smile curled at one corner of his wide, sensual mouth, but his eyes were cold. 'If it was done in an attempt to persuade me of your sterling qualities as a mother, it was misguided.' Again the unmistakable challenge in those deep grey eyes, and Cathy bit back the heated words of rebuttal. She couldn't trust herself to speak without getting her tongue in a tangle and could have boiled herself in oil for drinking all that sherry — not to mention the wine.

Hoping he would put her silence down to a refusal to dignify his snide remark with any comment at all, she rose from her seat, wobbled alarmingly as her head began to spin, and sat straight down again, only to hear his dry, sarcastic, 'For Juan's sake, I hope he is not in need of your ministrations tonight. If he is, then might I suggest you call Rosa out of her enforced retirement?'

Drunk in charge of a baby! Cathy thought, her head whirling. The hateful wretch had probably done it on purpose, feeding her one innocuous-looking measure of alcohol after another, inviting her opinion in that suave, wickedly sexy voice of his, intent on giving himself the proof that she wasn't a fit mother for an earthworm — let alone his nephew!

How she regained her feet and got herself to the door in more or less a straight line, she never knew. She even managed a stiff 'Goodnight' before he slewed round in his chair, one black brow tilted in sardonic enquiry as he questioned,

'Tell me, you say your name is Cathy, so why do your colleagues and friends know you as Cordy — or

Cordelia?' A very slight shrug, an even slighter smile. 'I am sure there is a logical reason, but I don't like puzzles. So humour me.'

Cathy could only stare at him, her eyes going so wide that they began to ache. He suspected; she knew he did. Had he waited until her fuddled brain would be incapable of thinking up some credible lie? Was that another of his devious reasons for systematically getting her drunk?

Somehow her tongue had got fused to the roof of her mouth, and her heart, tripping with alarm, didn't help her to think clearly, and his smile had a definite feral quality as he added with a cool politeness that made her skin crawl, 'Perhaps your memory requires a little help.' White teeth glittered between those sensual lips. 'After I read those letters, particularly the second, telling of the existence of my brother's alleged son, I made a few initial enquiries. I found the signature indecipherable, as you recall, but my description, my reminders of the party to mark the end of the assignment you were part of, all produced the same name. Cordelia Soames. Or Cordy to her friends — who, I might say, seemed to be numerous and almost exclusively male and, practically to a man. . .intimate.'

If nothing else could have sobered her, the hateful inflexion he placed on that last word did the trick. How dared he make her sister out to be a tramp, happy to fall in bed with anything in trousers? Cordy simply loved the reflected glamour of her job, the glitzy parties and socialising. And flirting was just a game to her, had been since she was fifteen years old. She wasn't promiscuous, not really. Surely the fact that she had got pregnant pointed to that? If she'd been in the habit of sleeping around she would have made sure she was protected.

Her head now miraculously clear, Cathy gave him a

withering smile, her voice dripping with acid as she told him, 'Far be it from me to allow you to lose any sleep over such a tricky puzzle, *señor*. Cordelia was my professional name. I thought plain old Cathy a little too homespun. Satisfied?'

He would have to be, she thought as she swept out of the door. He would have to come up with better trick questions than that before he caught her out— tipsy or sober. She was getting quite expert at the game of deceit!

Cathy closed her eyes against the brilliant white dry heat and pulled the shady brim of the floppy straw hat Rosa had lent her further down over her face.

She had hitched a ride on a tractor with Rafael, the eldest of Paquita and Tomás's brood, right to the edge of the vineyards, and now she set her sights on the shade offered by the grove of parasol pines she could see in the distance.

Behind her the tractor roared out of sight, leaving a cloud of white dust on the still air—the dust of the *Albariza* soil which made this vast triangle, stretching between the sherry towns of Jerez, Puerto de Santa María and Sanlúcar de Barrameda and encompassed by the rivers Guadalquivir and Guadalete, the one place in the world where the unique wine could be produced. So much she had learned from Rosa, who had been determined to educate as well as befriend her, Cathy thought with a quirky smile.

In fact her unexpected sense of relaxation was probably due as much to Rosa's friendship, the way she had taken pains to tell her so much about the area, as to the absence of Campuzano.

Not that he had left the *finca*; he hadn't. But he dined out every night. With his mother, Rosa said, but, with a cynicism that had appeared out of nowhere,

Cathy had expressed her doubts. The lady he dined with so regularly would be many years younger than Dona Luisa, the relationship between them certainly not that of mother and son!

And the rancour she felt when, ears straining, she heard the sounds of his return in the early hours of each morning was entirely due to the way he had insisted on dragging her away from home only to forget her existence, and the purpose of the visit — the introduction of the baby to his grandmother — which was seemingly just as far away as it had ever been.

Not that he had forgotten Johnny's existence, of course. A day never ended without him making time, usually before he disappeared out into the vineyards or into his study, to play with the child, his smile, the laughter and the affection in his eyes very real. And the chilliness when he met her eyes was real, too. And something else, something she had recognised as a muted enquiry, as if he were seeking an answer to a question that was beginning to annoy him.

Mentally she shrugged away the memory of the puzzled look she had surprised in his level grey glance only this morning, and stepped carefully over the cattle-grid. Spring flowers painted swaths of colour over the short green grass, delighting her artist's eye, the extravagant scarlet of the poppies and gold of the broom warming her heart. It was impossible to remain on edge and gloomy in this beautiful, bountiful part of Andalusia. Already she was beginning to love the area, feel at home and, for a couple of hours while the baby slept — with Rosa on hand to go to him should he wake — she was on the look-out for scenes which she could translate to paint and canvas when she and Johnny returned home.

She couldn't afford to be completely idle, and since she had taken over the responsibility of the baby she had needed to re-think her method of working. Bundling him into his buggy, she had searched out little-known areas of the capital, making quick preliminary sketches, taking a few photographs, and jotting down detailed colour notes.

Working with these *aides-mémoires* hadn't been as difficult as she had supposed at first, and what she could do in London she could do here. She had to do it; it was as simple as that. The cheque for the commissioned painting she had been putting the finishing touches to when Javier Campuzano had arrived in her life like an unexploded bomb had enabled her to pay a couple of months' rent in advance on her flat, bank enough to settle any outstanding bills that she might find waiting for her, and bring a little with her for emergencies. And that was all.

Shifting the strap of the canvas bag that held her equipment higher on to her shoulder, she strode towards the grove of pines, the slight breeze moulding the filmy material of her calf-length dress to her body. Cordy's jaw would drop, and stay dropped, with sheer amazement if she could see her now!

A couple of years ago, before that fateful party in Seville, Cordy had paid one of her increasingly rare visits to the small but exclusive apartment Cathy had rented near the agency.

'Here, you can have this,' Cordy had stated, tossing a gauzy bundle out of the suitcase she'd been unpacking in the tiny spare room. 'Though I don't suppose you'll ever wear it; you're too prim and proper and maiden-auntish. So take it to Oxfam, if you can be bothered.'

'Thanks a bundle,' Cathy replied drily, holding the garment out at arm's length.

The soft cream-coloured fabric was almost transparent, the style of the dress loose and floating, sleeveless with tiny seed-pearl buttons from the hem to the top of the deceptively demure neckline. It was beautiful, and obviously expensive, and Cordy dismissed, 'It's too "flower-power" for me. I don't know what possessed me to buy it.'

And Cathy hadn't worn it, but she hadn't given it away, either. She always chose sensible, hard-wearing, sober clothes because they suited her lifestyle and her image of herself as the pale shadow of her glamorous sister. She had kept it because it was beautiful, and frivolous, and when Campuzano had told her to pack cool clothing for her visit she had included the dress because the only light things she possessed were cotton trousers and a few cotton blouses.

And it was quite amazing how the drift of the soft, filmy fabric against her skin made her feel so feminine, as if her flesh were melting, becoming one with the soft, scented breeze, the fierce caress of the Andalusian sun. She certainly didn't feel prim and proper or in the least like a maiden aunt. But, to be fair, Cordy must have seen her that way.

In her own defence, however, if she'd seemed to be staid and careful, then it was because she'd had responsibility thrust upon her at an early age. Ten yers ago she'd been a normal fifteen-year-old, a little more studious than most, because she'd been determined to get herself qualified to follow a career in commercial art. And then the storm that was to change her life — all their lives — had broken. Her father, never a communicative man, had suddenly announced that he was leaving for South America. With another woman.

Her mother had been understandably shattered. She had never recovered from the shock and instead of leaning on her husband she had leaned on Cathy both emotionally and practically. And when Cordy had started to run wild it had been Cathy who'd had to wave the big stick, lay down the rules, and make sure they were kept.

Sinking to the dry earth beneath the welcome shade of the parasol pines, Cathy pushed such backward-looking thoughts to the far reaches of her mind and watched a tiny lizard with jewel-like eyes creep around the rough-textured trunk and then disappear with a flick of its tail, as if a magician had waved a wand.

Then, smiling, she got to her feet and wandered to the edge of the grove. Beyond, the *campos* stretched for mile after rolling mile. The soil, on this part of the *finca*, was not suitable for the vines and was given over to wheat, some olive groves and, inevitably, the raising of cattle and the breeding of horses.

Now, if she walked the gentle slope to the top of the nearest rounded hill, she would probably gain a wonderful vista encompassing the dark evergreen pines and dappled shade of the grove, the endless vineyards and, way, way in the distance, the view of the house. It might just make a wonderful painting.

Less than halfway up her feet dragged to a halt. She was hot and out of breath and should have had the sense to bring a bottle of water with her, because unless she encountered Rafael, or one of the other workers with a vehicle, she was going to have a long walk back to the farmhouse.

And Cathy, who didn't believe in miracles, gave thanks for what appeared to be just that as a horse and rider picked their way around the curving flank of the hill. He had probably been riding round the cattle, checking fences or whatever, and, in this heat, he would surely carry water with him.

Not that she was in danger of dying of thirst, she told herself. But she was parched and just a few sips would give her the energy to get herself up to the top of this hill and then back to the farmhouse.

She sieved through the few words of Spanish she had picked up around Paquita and Tomás. *Agua*. Yes, that was it. Water. The solitary, dust-covered rider was closer now, close enough to hear the creak of saddle leather, and she raised her arm, calling out, '*Hola!*'

The rider made no response, merely sat his horse as if he were part of it as the beautiful white animal picked its way daintily towards her. He was wearing a straight-brimmed black Cordoban hat, tipped forward a little to shade his eyes, rough black denim covered his broad chest and perfectly straight back, and his long legs were covered by protective leather chaps. There was something very macho, deeply sexy about these Spanish men, Cathy thought, surprising herself, and then felt her whole body turn to fire as she recognised those tanned, grave features, that sensual mouth. . .

'*Hola!*' He returned her greeting, reining in the big stallion as he drew level. The wide mouth curled in a smile as she took a hasty step back, her heart still pattering over the unwelcome recognition that she found Campuzano the sexiest man alive. But she lifted her head bravely and, deep in the shade of the straight black brim, she caught the grey glitter of his eyes. And sexual awareness, such as she had never known, sliced through her like a knife, making her incapable of thought, let alone speech, as he asked, his fantastic voice soft and taunting, 'Lost, Cathy? Surely not?' And when she merely shook her head, 'Or were you looking for me?'

'Of course not. Why should I do that?' She was back in control again. Just. He might be the most attractive man she had ever set eyes on—and why had the realisation battered her with such sudden and unwanted force?—but he was also the most dangerous. She knew he would take Johnny from her if he could, sparing her feelings not a single thought.

'Why indeed?' His voice was a touch sarcastic, but then she was used to that. And she couldn't read his expression, because he turned his head as he dismounted. And if he thought she'd trigged herself up and come looking for him. . . She bit her lip, wishing she hadn't worn this wretched dress.

On his feet, he hitched the reins over the pommel of the heavy, high-backed saddle and, turning his head, glinted down at her.

'What did you want? A ride back to the house?'

'No.' She dragged in a big deep breath. She wasn't exactly a dwarf herself, but, standing so close, he towered above her, overwhelming her with all that raw male virility, the scent of his skin mingling with the scents of leather and hot white dust and sunlight.

Agitatedly, she fiddled with the strap of her canvas bag, hauling it higher on her shoulder. She had enough trouble holding her own with him over the question of Johnny's future, plus the ever increasing hassle with her conscience over all those lies she had been forced into telling, without her wretched hormones starting to play up.

She simply couldn't afford to allow the main and very serious issue of her long-term plan to legally adopt the baby to get sidelined or clouded by this awful, enervating and shockingly sudden sexual awareness.

Stay calm, she ordered herself. If she could fight his take-over bid for the child she could fight her own hormones; of course she could. And she pleasantly surprised herself by answering coldly, 'I didn't recognise you at first and I'm perfectly able to get myself back to the house. But I would like a drink—water, if you have it.'

'But of course.' His hand gripped her elbow lightly and the effect of the electrical jolt produced by that small, almost impersonal gesture traumatised her all over again so that she was scarcely aware of her feet touching the ground as he led her down to the shady pine grove.

The big white stallion followed like a lamb at Campuzano's soft whistle — no need for a heavy hand on the reins when the Jerezano was around, Cathy thought on a flash of pique that went quite a long way towards bringing her back down to earth. When the master lifted an eyebrow everyone jumped, including the horse!

Once again the cool scent of the pines enfolded her like a blessing as her feet sank into the soft, dry earth, but this time round Cathy was feeling far from relaxed, because she now knew that the edginess she unfailingly felt in his company had more to it than divided opinions over the baby's future.

'Share my lunch,' he invited, unbuckling a saddle-pack. 'Sit down; make yourself comfortable.'

So Cathy obstinately remained standing, just to show him that there happened to be someone around who didn't immediately and automatically do exactly as he said. But he appeared not to notice, taking a cloth-covered bundle from the pack, extracting a flask, and tossing it in her direction, telling her, his voice uninterested, 'Help yourself. You didn't choose the most sensible time of day to walk in the hills. I hope you used plenty of sunblock.'

'Of course. I'm not a fool.' She unstoppered the flask. 'I won't come out in blisters and put you to the trouble of having to give me care and attention.' The beat-up container had long since lost its plastic cup, and she shrugged slightly, lifting it to her mouth and drinking deeply. The vacuum flask had kept the water deliciously cool and fresh and she lowered it reluctantly, the tip of her tongue coming out to lap the last shining droplets from her lips.

And she found him watching her, the amusement in his eyes making her wary, because she didn't know what he was finding funny until he said, 'That isn't what I meant. But is it what you feel?' The end of a long forefinger deliberately tipped the straight brim of his hat, pushing it further back on his head, revealing all the warmth of those fascinating grey eyes. 'You consider I don't give you enough care and attention?'

'Is that supposed to be a serious question?' Furious with the colour she felt crawl over her face, Cathy sat down on the ground, tucking her legs beneath her, removing herself a little way from the unsettling nearness of him. Of course she didn't want more of his attention. Why should she? For some reason it wasn't a subject she wanted to pursue, and she changed it quickly.

'I use the afternoons to explore because it's the one time of the day I can be sure Johnny will nap for an hour or so. Rosa's around if he should wake, but I'm invariably back before he does. Talking of which. . .' She gathered herself, beginning to get back on her feet. 'It's time I was going.'

'Stay.' It was an order, the quiet, not-to-be-argued-with tone reinforced by the touch of his hand on her arm. Merely a touch, but enough to set up a quivering reaction in her naked flesh. Cathy tensed, denying the instinct to snatch her arm away, scramble to her feet, and run. She wasn't stupid enough to alert him to the way he affected her. 'You have no need to try so hard to convince me of your maternal devotion.'

He hunkered down at her side, withdrawing his hand, setting her free to come back with, 'I have no need to try to be devoted to Johnny, believe me.' Tartly said, and putting that look of query back in his eyes, his gaze level, his mouth compressing a little as he asked her,

'You're managing to resist the temptation to take up your former career?'

He was so transparent in this one respect. She could have laughed in his face, but resisted the impulse. Her supposed need for the bright lights and glamour had been something he'd banked on, the one sure way to get her to agree to hand Johnny's legal guardianship over to the father's side of the child's family.

Of course, his reasoning was spot-on — how spot-on he would never discover if she had her way. But he'd got hold of the wrong woman, and it never ceased to amaze her that a man with his undoubted experience with the opposite sex could, for one moment, believe her to be model material. And her eyes were unconsciously sparkling at him as she riposted, 'Sorry to disappoint you, Javier. But I have two new careers to concentrate on. Motherhood and painting.'

And you'd better believe it, she added inside her head, and met an unreadable look in his eyes and heard him say, 'We make progress. It is the first time you have used my name.'

Was it? She supposed it must be. She looked away quickly, trying to find something to say that would counter the possibility of his believing she was seeking some level of intimacy with him. And found it, telling him, 'I really have to get back. It won't be too long before he wakes. Thanks for the drink.'

'You will reach him more quickly if you ride back with me.' Dark eyes compelled her to acknowledge the truth of that. And an outright refusal on her part would tell him, more surely than anything, that she couldn't cope with his company. So she merely shrugged and accepted the slice of cold potato omelette he handed her on the tip of a wicked-looking knife.

The thick *tortilla* was full of flavour, more than satisfying, but she couldn't resist the thin slice of ham he offered, obviously reading the beginnings of denial in her eyes because he stated, 'The best ham in the country is produced in Andalusia. I insist you try it.'

'Lovely.' Licking her fingers, she felt almost stupidly relaxed, her eyes half closed as she watched his strong, capable fingers deal with the knife, flicking the wicked blade back inside its protective covering, before he leaned back and stretched out beside her, his arms crossed behind his head.

Her hands clasped around her knees, Cathy turned to look at him, the single braid of long blonde hair falling forward over her shoulder. Mentally, she had put him at around thirty-seven or -eight, but now, stretched out on the warm earth, wearing dust-stained working clothes, he looked a good five years younger. And he looked, as ever, magnificent. The black hat covered his face, and the slow, regular rise and fall of his chest made her decide he was asleep. And for once she was in no hurry at all to get back to the farmhouse before Johnny woke. Rosa was there, not to mention Paquita, and Johnny had a generous heart; he already loved both of them.

And it was so peaceful here, no sound but the chirp of the crickets in the grass, the very slightest whisper of wind as it winnowed through the swaying scarlet poppies. Her entire body felt as if it had no more substance than melted honey.

Even out of the blistering sunlight the still air beneath the pines was heady and warm. Her fingers crept with slow, unthinking languor to the buttons at the high round neckline of her filmy dress, undoing two, then three, making little flapping movements with the diaphanous fabric, lazily trying to create and capture a tiny cooling breeze, and Javier said drowsily, 'Let me help you.'

CHAPTER FOUR

JAVIER'S voice was like a lazy drift of smoke, curling gently in the warm scented air, stroking her, making her lose touch with reality because, for a start, she had never felt this relaxed before, never felt quite so dreamy.

His big, lean body idled over, the hat flipped aside, his head propped on one hand, the other hand lifting, almost in slow motion, his warm fingers tucking inside the gauzy cream fabric, sliding another button away from its unsafe anchorage, and yet another. . .

Cathy was mesmerised and wondered, vaguely, what had happened to all those inhibitions her sister had accused her of having. Had they thawed in the hot Spanish sun, revealing a woman capable of the sensuality that openly welcomed and enjoyed the caress of the back of a man's fingers against the full, soft globes of her breasts?

Not any man, of course, she thought on a wave of bewilderment. Just this man, this one man.

His lean, sexy body inched closer with a whisper of leather against denim, and she closed her eyes, inhaling the virile scent of leather and dust and heat and man. And wondered why she had never felt this way before, as if her whole body were melting, becoming nothing more than an object created for this man's pleasure, a wantonly willing receptacle for his passion.

Tiny shocked voices pricked at the back of her oddly bemused mind as, the buttons dealt with — every last one of them — Javier stroked the edges of her dress aside. And those shocked little voices just might have

won as she felt his breath catch in his throat and
opened her eyes to find his making a lazy, appreciative
inventory of her nearly naked body.

No man had ever seen her like this before. When
she and Donald had made love it had, on both unmem-
orable occasions, happened in the quick and fumbling
dark.

Her skin tensed, the beginnings of shame, of a
desperate repudiation, gathering now. And with it a
sense of loss, a deep regret, because the inhibitions
were clamouring back, crowding out all that wonderful,
unthinking, delicious sensuality. But a tiny, unnoticed
movement had the front fastening of her lacy bra
undone, had her full bounty falling into the sensual
cups of his hands, and the tiny repressive voices were
drowned out in the thunder of her heartbeats, the
raging heat of her blood as it took fire in her veins.

'Bella. . . Bella. . .' She could have drowned in the
sweet, soft warmth of that voice, and she did, her
breath coming in small panting gasps as he dipped his
dark head to lap his tongue with languid satisfaction
over the proud peak of each taut nipple in turn, again
and again until she thought she would die from the
sweet torture.

She reached for his head, her taut fingers digging
through the soft dark hair, finding the hardness of bone
as she sank further and further into mindless oblivion,
down and down towards the mystery that was as old as
time. And he lifted his head from the deep valley of
her pouting breasts and slowly, so slowly, drew the tip
of one sinfully expert finger down over the centre of
her ribcage, on and on over the soft curve of her
stomach, hovering lightly at the edge of her lacy briefs.

His name was a wild, unspoken cry on her trembling
lips as she instinctively arched her spine and heard,

through the tumult of her heartbeats, his softly spoken, 'Such a multiplicity of talents. . .'

And knew what he was implying.

Cathy went hot with shame, then cold with the knowledge of how she had allowed herself to be used. Bastard! Oh, the *bastard*!

He'd been referring to her supposed prowess in bed. How could she tell him that this sort of thing had never, ever happened to her before? She couldn't, and even if she did he wouldn't believe her. His lovemaking had been a honey-baited trap, yet another weapon to prove her to be an unsuitable mother for his brother's son.

Jerking her knees up, she twisted away, fumbling for the maddeningly elusive front fastening of her bra, her face on fire.

'*Por Dios*!' The ragged words slashed through the thick, warm silence, and Cathy swallowed a scream. Was he trying to make her think he had been just as involved, just as lost in those long moments of intimacy as she?

Well, she knew better. It had been simply an evil ploy to prove she was little better than a whore. Ratfink!

'Don't you touch me again. Ever!' she commanded hoarsely, sniffing, almost crying because all those tiny buttons, all eight million of them, refused to obey her fingers and slot into the right holes! And he was standing now, and her furious eyes met the grey grimness of his and she looked away again, quickly, knowing that if she stopped feeling angry she would die of embarrassment.

Her dress buttoned, she hoped correctly, she tried to shake some of the rumples out of the gauzy fabric and cast around for Rosa's hat, jammed it on her head, and marched away, her shoulders very straight, leaving him doing something with his horse.

How could she have behaved so. . .so. . .? Well, she wouldn't think about it now. If she did, then the tears of embarrassed humiliation and shame she could feel welling up in her eyes would begin to fall in earnest. And her pride wouldn't let her walk back into the farmhouse, passing numerous vineyard workers on the way, her face all blotched from a crying jag. And she stiffened, almost falling over herself, as his cold voice rang out, '*Ven acá*! You ride back with me.'

She'd sooner die!

But the sound of hoof-beats told her she had little option, and the arm that scooped her into the saddle in front of the Jerezano made a nonsense of her attempts to wriggle free, and the no doubt colourful Spanish expletive he gritted against her ear reinforced her knowledge of the danger her struggles were putting them in as he cantered the powerful stallion across the poppy-strewn field and, with a muscular command of his hard thighs, put the animal at the gate at the side of the cattle-grid.

Tension released as the graceful, arching leap ended with the thrum of hoof-beats in the white dust, all the fight leaving her in a whoosh of air, leaving her forlornly aware of the heat of his body against her back, the hard nudge of his thighs behind her own.

Cathy gritted her teeth, trying to blot out all those sensations. The one man she should have kept at a coolly polite distance was the only man she had ever allowed such liberties. Somehow she was going to have to live with that, and with him, for the next few weeks. She didn't know how she would manage it.

How he would gloat as he chalked up yet another black mark against her.

But there was nothing gloating in the severity of his

expression as he reined in the horse at the entrance to the courtyard, dismounted, and helped her down. She should be grateful, she supposed numbly as her feet hit the ground and he withdrew his hands from her waist at once, that he hadn't ridden straight into the courtyard in full view of Paquita, Tomás and any of the others that happened to be around.

She would have made her escape, but, with dignity, couldn't. She was blocked in by his body, the horse and the courtyard wall. And he was going to come out with something to humiliate her further — if that were possible — she just knew it.

Trying to be brave, to face whatever he cared to throw at her, she lifted her chin and met his stony features. His eyes glittered beneath the black brim of his hat and Cathy shuddered, fighting to hang on to the courage that told her she would slap him if he said one word out of turn. One word. . .

But, despite her determination to stare him down, one of all those pent-up tears escaped, slithered shamefully down her cheek, making her hang her head. She couldn't bear him to witness the state he'd so cruelly brought her to. And then she heard the drag of his indrawn breath, quick and sharp, as if tears were the very last thing he had expected to see. And he moved away, re-mounting, touching his hand to the brim of his hat as the horse moved away on dancing hoofs, his voice abrasive as he uttered, 'It is time we talked. Until then, *adiós.*'

'The *señor* is back.' Rosa spoke in a lisping whisper, tiptoeing over the carpet to where Cathy stood, looking down at the sleeping baby. 'He asked me to tell you to dine with him tonight. Nine o'clock.'

Oh, God! Cathy turned quickly to make unnecessary adjustments to the wooden louvres at the windows, hiding the way her colour came and went. Javier had been away for three days; she hadn't seen him since he'd left her outside the courtyard. As far as she was concerned he could have stayed away forever and, as for having dinner with him, she simply didn't think she could bear it.

Three days hadn't made her feel less ashamed of her wanton behaviour. What must he think of her? But, more importantly, what did she think of herself?

'Está bien?' Rosa prodded, and Cathy turned, making herself smile.

'Yes, it's all right. You'll keep an eye on Johnny for me?'

No need to ask. Rosa adored the baby. She smiled and confirmed in a whisper, 'Of course. Any time, you know that.' Her eyes glowed as she peeped into the crib. 'Me, I am not modern, like my sisters. One is studying law and another is a translator in Brussels — but you already know this. I guess I'm old-fashioned; all I want is to marry and have dozens of babies! And you?' The big brown eyes were doleful now. 'One day you will marry, too. Have more babies.' Her fingers walked lightly over the soft blanket covering the sleeping baby. 'It was so sad for you that Don Francisco died. But one day you will find someone who will take his place in your heart.'

Cathy turned away quickly, her long blonde hair falling forward to hide her face. She hated having to live with lies, especially where Rosa and her family were concerned, and now, in the face of all this unearned sympathy, she was deeply tempted to tell the truth. And if it weren't for the vexed question of Johnny's future, she would have done. As it was, she could only say, her voice gruff, 'Maybe. Thanks for the message. I suppose I should get changed.'

Not that it would take a full hour to get ready to

have dinner with Javier, she reflected crossly as Rosa
walked quietly out, promising to look in on Johnny
from time to time. She didn't want to have to spend
time with him and she didn't know how she would
endure a dinner that, if the former occasion was
anything to go by, could stretch out for a couple of
hours at least.

But she had no option but to obey the royal command. To refuse would only serve to alert him to her
emotional muddle, and he would be perceptive enough
to guess that memories of what had happened in the
pine grove had tormented her for the past three days,
her nights made sleepless with haunting recollections
of the way he had made her feel.

The only way she could hope to handle seeing him
again was to pretend the episode had never happened.
That he might construe that, for her, such sexual
encounters were practically everyday occurrences,
earning no place in her memory because there were so
many of them, was a risk she was going to have to
take.

She showered quickly and dressed in a plain blue
cotton skirt and a sleeveless darker blue blouse, braid-
ing her hair and twisting it round her head like a
coronet. He wouldn't be able to complain that her
appearance insulted his dinner-table, and neither, more
importantly, could he accuse her of dressing to tease.

The knot in her stomach twisted unbearably as she
went to join him but, just over an hour later, when he
instructed Paquita to take their coffee out to the
courtyard, it had gone completely.

Just at the beginning, when he'd offered her a glass
of *fino* — which she had instantly and coolly refused —
she had been at her wits' end to know how to control
the immediate and shocking need she had been utterly
swamped by. The need to feel his lips, his hands, his

eyes on her body again, to recapture the glorious sensations he had so effortlessly created in the soft shade of the pine trees.

She had felt her face, her whole body, crawl with colour and had had to twist her hands together until her knuckles showed white through the lightly tanned skin to stop them from shaking. But if he'd noticed he made no comment and, throughout the meal, he had acted as if nothing had ever happened between them, telling her he had spent the last three days in Seville, on business, describing the city, the museums, the fashionable shops, all the things any visitor would want to see.

He was polite and impersonal, his unforced sophistication soothing her, a world apart from the dust-stained gaucho-figure of the *campos*. And that helped.

'And if you visit Sevilla — and I don't see why you shouldn't manage it during your time here — you must sit at a table with a glass of wine in the Plaza del Triunfo and gaze at the Giralda, the world's most beautiful minaret,' he told her as he escorted her out to the courtyard.

'The evening would be best; do as the Sevillanos do — take a stroll and people-watch.'

'Sounds fun,' Cathy was now relaxed enough to comment, not bothering to tell him that such a jaunt was highly unlikely, that she had a child to care for and precious little money. A suspicion formed in her mind that maybe he was trying to get rid of her, for some no doubt devious reasons of his own, but she mentally brushed it aside as she sat at the table against the courtyard wall which dripped with purple bougainvillaea. Just one cup of coffee and then she could, without seeming impolite, bring the evening to an end, with nothing unpleasant or contentious said by either of them. She reached for the pot.

But Javier proved how wrong she was, stunning her. 'I would like to formally adopt Juan, bring him up here, as an Andaluz—— No, hear me out,' he commanded with quiet courtesy as she opened her mouth to refuse to contemplate such a thing. 'He needs to be part of his heritage, to live with it and grow with it, to be taught how to handle the responsibilities of the business empire that will one day belong to him. Not just the vineyards and *bodegas*, but the Campuzano interests in wheat, olives, cattle and horses, hotels and foreign investments. As I have told you, Francisco's son is my heir. He would not thank you if, in later years, he were to gain his inheritance, not knowing how to begin to handle it.' His dark grey eyes were sombre beneath his level brows, as if he were intent on imprinting his will on her own.

Cathy held herself very still. There was a chill in her bones, despite the soft warmth of the purple night. And his voice was dark with the slow threat of inevitability as he placed his convictions before her, emphasised them.

'I have excellent managers to look after the day-to-day running of various enterprises. But in the end the buck stops with the head of the family. There are decisions to be made, sometimes difficult, even vital. And to make them wisely the head of the family, at any given time, has to know exactly what he is doing. Do you understand what I am saying to you?'

Cathy was trying hard not to. She said quickly, too sharply, 'Johnny has an English heritage, too. Or would you rather forget that?' Knowing full well he would. His Andalusian pride would completely dismiss the English mother who had given birth to his nephew as no account. With, as he believed, a second-rate modelling career behind her and a doubtful artistic one in front of her, why should she enter into the equation at all?

'Of course not,' he denied, far too smoothly. 'Juan would be educated in England, as both Francisco and I were. And of course, if you wished, you could stay here to be with him, satisfy yourself that he is getting all the care and love he needs — and I can assure you he will have that, in abundance. And it goes without saying that I would ensure you were well provided for, financially.' He leant against the back of his seat, the soft lights from the house not touching his face. One hand idly stirred the coffee that had gone cold in his cup. 'What do you say?'

'No.'

See her darling baby taken over by this — this coldhearted despot, by a grandmother who hadn't yet been able to bring herself even to look at him? Never! And she could stay here, could she? Pushed up a corner, kept out of sight, helplessly standing by while Johnny's future was minutely mapped out, step by pre-ordained step. No way!

'Señor,' she managed, hanging on to her dignity with difficulty, 'I may not be able to give Johnny the financial advantages you could, but I can give him everything else he needs — including a future career of his own choosing. I am his — his mother.' Her tongue stumbled guiltily on the lie. 'I won't hand him over to you. But,' she offered quickly, because to do otherwise would send him straight to the courts, 'I will agree to let you see him whenever you're in London and bring him here for holidays when he is old enough to understand that he is partly Spanish.'

He said nothing. And the long silence was blistering. It said far more than any words could have done. It unnerved her completely and when she could stand it no longer she jerked to her feet and Javier stood, too, his lean height overwhelming her with its steely strength, and his breath fanned her cheek as he stated calmly, 'Then I will marry you. Please sit down.'

Cathy did. She had no choice. Her legs gave way. Marry him?

Re-seating himself, this time on the opposite side of the table, the courtyard lights at his back making his expression impossible to see, he confessed, 'When I first sought you out in London I was sure you could be bought off, sure you would choose freedom and financial inducements over the problems and sacrifices of single-parenthood. But you have proved me wrong.' The quiet amazement of his tone would have amused her, had things been different. As it was, she trembled helplessly. And he continued with soft yet devastating determination, 'I am prepared, for Juan's sake, to marry you and formally adopt Juan as my own son. For selfish and fairly obvious reasons, I would rather it hadn't come to this. However. . .' The shrug of wide shoulders that owed nothing to expensive tailoring was slight enough to have been missed. 'Rationally, our marriage would be the ideal solution to the problem. And of course——' he rose fluidly to his feet '—the marriage would be in name only. Come. . .' He extended a hand. 'I will walk you to your room. You are cold.'

She wasn't. Tension was making her shiver. But she stood up anyway, ignoring his hand, carefully keeping her distance as they walked across the courtyard, biting back an innner scream as he remarked conversationally, 'Married to me, you would have the protection of my name and Juan would be legitimised. But you must think very carefully before you answer. As my wife, your reputation would have to be beyond reproach. Could you contemplate a chaste future?'

As there could be no question of their marrying,

Cathy didn't reply. They reached the door to her room in silence and she would have walked straight through, but he adroitly blocked her way.

'Tomorrow we go to stay in Jerez so that my mother can get acquainted with her grandson. I would like your answer by the morning. If you agree, we can break the news to her at once. She is very traditional in her outlook and would feel happier if she knew Juan was to be legitimised. And I'm afraid I have to warn you that, if your answer is no, then I shall go through every court available to me to gain legal custody of my brother's child.'

For the first time since he had made his insulting proposal of marriage, she looked at him in full light. His features were grave, courteous even. But his eyes were cold.

Cathy had never felt so alone and frightened in her life.

CHAPTER FIVE

'How much time will you need?' Although his voice was low, mindful of Rosa in the back seat with Johnny, there was a bite of impatience in his tone. It jerked Cathy reluctantly back to face reality.

Defensively, she had been concentrating on what she could see of the old quarter of Jerez, her only acknowledgement of Javier's presence coming in the form of a vague admiration for the way he handled the big car, negotiating the narrow warren of streets with a confidence she could only envy.

Amazingly, she had slept well last night, dismissing Javier's cold-blooded proposal, because there was no point in giving it a second thought. Even if she had been the baby's natural mother she would never have considered tying herself to a man who wanted marriage merely because it would tidy things up. She would never willingly sentence herself to the type of barren life he had promised, a life devoid of affection, of love, respect and companionship.

And, as she wasn't Johnny's mother, merely his aunt, his proposal was doubly damned, did he but know it. If she agreed to the marriage, merely for the baby's sake of course, then her lies would be right out in the open and Javier Campuzano would move in for the kill.

All she could do was play for time, and when he'd asked her for her decision this morning she'd stuck a pious expression on her face and told him she needed more time before she could make a decision of such magnitude. She was either going to have to sneak

71

herself and Johnny back to England — and quite how she'd manage that she didn't know, given that she didn't have enough money for the air fare and it wouldn't be exactly easy to 'sneak' a boisterous baby and half a ton of impedimenta out from under his aristocratic nose — or hold him at bay until the adoption went through. Somehow.

'Well?' The anger was barely contained, and Cathy said with a gleefully manufactured smarminess,

'I'm afraid I can't possibly commit myself to a definite time span. Sorry. But when I've reached a decision, you'll be the first to know.' And hoped his blood-pressure shot through the roof.

He wanted to placate his mother. Dona Luisa would be happier if the situation were regularised, if she could be told that her grandson would soon legitimately bear the revered Campuzano name. She had heard the Spaniards not only doted on their children, but on their mothers, too. No wonder he wanted his answer at once.

Tough!

Behind them the baby crowed, and Rosa, deployed to come with them as nursemaid, gave a tiny laughing shriek as she tried to disentangle small fingers from her curly black hair, and Javier brought the car to a suave halt in front of a studded black door roughly halfway down the narrow, shady alleyway.

A closed door. It looked as if it hadn't been opened in centuries. A few windows in the high plain walls, all adorned with the ornamental protective iron *rejas*. No sign of the welcome mat, Cathy thought, pushing out a stubborn chin. But then she hadn't expected one, had she? She was no better than she should be, had brought shame on the family name, and only if she was prepared to enter Javier's plans for a cover-up could she expected to be tolerated, let alone welcomed.

She had once read, somewhere, that Spaniards put women into two categories: madonnas or whores. Modern thinking in this vital, go-ahead country would have reliquished such outdated conceptions. But not, she was sure, where the old, wealthy families were concerned, especially among those of Dona Luisa's generation. Their attitudes would be firmly rooted in the old traditions, and Cathy knew which category she would come in!

Oh, Cordy, she mourned silently, not for the first time, see what a mess you have got me into!

And Javier grunted, none too pleasantly, 'Help Rosa with the child and the immediate essentials while I find someone to unload and park the car.' And he left her sitting there, feeling about as wanted as a tax demand, watching as he slotted a huge iron key into the large, forbidding door.

Nothing for it but to follow. She slid her long legs out of the air-conditioned luxury of the Mercedes and, even in the shade of the tall buildings, the heat of the afternoon hit her. And that wasn't all that hit her. Panic punched at her chest, making her want to hitch up her skirts and run. But while she had Johnny she couldn't do that, and while she had Johnny she would find the strength to play the game her way, keep Javier at a distance, albeit a fuming one, while she waited until the the adoption—or, at the very least, a residence order—came through.

Taking the baby from Rosa, she held his warm, sturdy body against her shoulder and dropped loving kisses on the top of his downy head. She had loved and cared for him since his birth, and no one was going to take him from her.

Johnny blew a raspberry against the side of her neck then gurgled with laughter, and Cathy swallowed the lump in her throat, hoisted him higher into her arms, and told him, 'Let's go find Granny, sweetheart. And what about a nice bowl of oatmeal and a squashed-up banana?'

Johnny blew another raspberry and Cathy gave him a brief cuddle before following Rosa and the baby baggage through that intimidating door. Then she stood stock-still, her eyes going very wide as someone slid out of the door, closing it, leaving her staring at a scene that was pure magic.

They were in a courtyard. A series of arches formed shady cloisters on three sides and, in the centre of the immaculate ancient paving, water played in a marble fountain. All around, in pots and urns and terracotta bowls, were flowers in abundance — roses, stately lilies, white geraniums and sweet-scented jasmine.

Cathy's eyes were wide, her soft mouth slightly open. It was so unexpected. She would never have imagined such an oasis of peace, of scented tranquillity, to exist behind such a plain, forbidding exterior. And the man who had gone out to the street came back in, loaded down with their luggage, and, ahead, beneath one of the arches, Rosa beckoned. Cathy gathered herself together, her stomach fluttering. Just for one timeless moment, wallowing in all the graceful legacy of the Moors, she had forgotten what was actually facing her.

The second great studded door was open, and Rosa led the way into a huge marble-paved hall. To one side ran a wide, shady passage with windows looking out on to the courtyard on one side, immense carved doors on the other. The man with the suitcases trudged up the sweeping marble staircase, the banisters of which were a miracle of decorative, delicate ironwork. And a woman came forward to meet them, small, bird-like, her olive-toned skin mapped with a thousand wrinkles. Dona Luisa? Cathy's heart shuddered. There was no sign of Javier.

Strangely enough, she wanted him at her side, craved his presence. She caught her breath, her arms tightening around Johnny. Only because she was in a strange place, her reception uncertain, to say the least. That was all, of course it was. And the meeting she had come to dread the more it had been postponed wasn't about to take place right now, she acknowledged with a sense of reprieve, because Rosa was introducing, 'Maria is Dona Luisa's housekeeper. I'm afraid she speaks very little English. If there's anything you need for yourself and baby, go through me.'

'*Buenas tardes*, Maria.' Cathy dredged up a smile for the housekeeper, to be met by a dip of the dark head in cool acknowledgement, and saw, with a kind of wonder, how a flame of joy was kindled in the still beautiful black eyes as they dismissed her and glanced to the squirming, dribbling baby.

There followed a veritable torrent of Spanish which Rosa loosely translated as they followed Maria up the magnificent shallow staircase.

'She is saying that Juan looks exactly as his father did at his age. She was nursemaid to both Don Javier and Don Francisco when they were babies. She would like to look after baby now. But I tell her that is my position. I guard it jealously!'

And just as well, Cathy thought. Juan—more and more, just recently, she had found herself thinking of her baby by his Spanish name—Johnny wouldn't know where he was at if he kept being handed to one minder after another. He knew and loved Rosa and, to be truthful, Cathy was mightily thankful that her Spanish friend had been instructed to accompany them. Not only for the baby's sake, but for her own. With Rosa around, in her corner, she wouldn't feel so alone and disorientated.

'Here we are,' Rosa said in her ear, and Cathy came

to a standstill as Maria flung open an elaborately carved wooden door and Rosa trotted through. It was a beautiful room, Cathy thought, following, but wasn't given time to take stock as the other girl dived through one of the two interior doors and announced importantly, 'The nursery. See? Don Javier told me he had given instructions. He knows you won't be separated from the little one.'

And indeed, the adjoining small room had been kitted out with everything a small child could need, just as had the tower room back at the *finca*. The Campuzanos, mother and son, had obviously not seen the baby's stay as fleeting!

But, however debatable that particular point, Cathy had to admit that having everything necessary right under her nose was a big bonus. And as Rosa began unpacking the bundles, laying out disposable nappies, clothes, tins of baby-food formula and packets of oatmeal, Cathy propped the baby up in his crib and plugged in the electric kettle to boil water to mix his feed.

'I'll go to the kitchen,' Rosa offered, 'and see if they've got such a thing as a nice ripe peach or banana, shall I?'

Almost every day the two of them had fun introducing new tastes — just tiny ones — into his diet, and Cathy nodded. 'Thanks. But if it's peach, only a very little. He hasn't tried it before. And I'll make up the oatmeal.'

Not that she needed to issue such warnings, Cathy reflected. Rosa was more than usually sensible for her age; she was lucky to have her around. Leaving the bottle to cool, she took Johnny on her knee as she sat in the nursing chair and changed him deftly. And, hearing the door open and close quietly behind her, she said, 'That was quick. He's ready for his meal.

What did you get?' and went completely still as an almost unaccented, mellifluous voice replied,

'You must be Cathy.'

Tensing all over, she made herself turn. Dona Luisa was dressed all in black, but elegantly, and the beauty of her bone-structure was astonishing. But more astonishing still was the warmth in the lovely grey eyes, the smile that came quickly as she bent to brush a soft, lightly perfumed cheek over Cathy's and told her, 'You must forgive me for not being on hand to greet you when you first arrived. But I'd most firmly instructed myself to keep out of the way until you and the baby were settled. But——' a mischievous moue made her look twenty years younger than her early sixties '—I couldn't keep away.' She pulled up a chair and sank on to it, and there was some kind of yearning in her eyes as she whispered to Cathy, 'May I?' and held out her hands to the baby.

'Oh, of course.' She handed him over with no compunction at all, her throat actually filling up with compassion when she saw the older woman's eyes grow decidedly misty as she cuddled the sturdy child against her elegantly clad shoulder.

'I can't tell you how happy I am,' Dona Luisa said, her voice wobbly. 'I never expected to hold a grandchild. Javier vowed he would never re-marry, and Francisco. . . Francisco died. But now. . .' She thrust dark thoughts away. 'Now I have this beautiful grandson.' She dropped half a dozen doting kisses on his beaming face. 'Tell me, my dear, what is your preference—Juan, or Johnny?'

Cathy's throat went tight with emotion: relief, gratitude, and goodness only knew what else. Never in her wildest dreams had she expected to be welcomed so pleasantly. She had, it appeared, worried about nothing. And she was actually having her preferences

deferred to. That made a change! The dictatorial Javier
had gone ahead and re-christened the baby whether
she liked it or not.

And Cathy answered softly, feeling unaccountably
humble, 'Juan—while he's in Spain.'

'Splendid!' There was no mistaking the warmth in
the lovely grey eyes, and the following two hours
passed in a haze of stunned amazement as, with much
laughter and a great deal of chatter, Dona Luisa stayed
to help with playtime and bath-time, right through to
the final feed for the night.

Not one disapproving word had been said or a look
that had been other than friendly been given. A pity
Javier could not be as warm and tolerant as his mother,
Cathy thought, wondering where the monster had got
to. It wasn't like him to miss his nephew's pre-bedtime
romps.

'He will learn both English and Spanish with his very
first words,' Dona Luisa whispered, her eyes lingering
on the almost asleep baby as Cathy tucked him into his
crib. 'He will be fluently bilingual before he goes to
school!'

Cathy found a smile from somewhere. It would be
months before Juan began to say his first coherent
words. He and she would be long gone before then.
But she couldn't bring herself to hurt the older woman.
She had lost both her husband and her younger son. If
she mistakenly believed that her grandson would be a
permanent part of her life, then the disillusionment
would have to wait for some other time.

Obviously reading Cathy's silence as a need for
quietness, Dona Luisa gave the drowsy child one last
loving look and walked softly from the room. Cathy
had no option but to follow, leaving the communicating
door open just a fraction, and the older woman whispered, 'I'll leave you to settle in now. If there's

anything you need — anything at all — you only have to ask. Oh, and we dine at ten — rather later than Javier does when he's at the *finca* — but I'll see you in the *sala* at nine. We'll take an aperitif together and have a good gossip.'

Dona Luisa was nothing like the ogre she'd come to expect, Cathy thought, her violet eyes bemused as she watched Javier's mother walk out of the door. And she couldn't imagine why he had insisted on delaying the meeting, keeping his mother away from the grandson she was obviously ready to dote on, allowing her, Cathy, to think the worst, believing that Dona Luisa was having to brace herself to meet the scarlet woman who had slept her way into their illustrious family!

She could have spent the entire six weeks of her stay in Spain quite happily here with Juan's charming grandmother. Her initial instincts had been right, she was sure. Dona Luisa would understand that the baby would be better off with his mother — well, his adoptive mother. And maybe as they got to know each other better she could even tell her the truth, explain that she, Cathy, loved the baby as if he were truly her own, that the thought of having to give him up, as Javier had threatened, was breaking her heart.

Dona Luisa would understand, and she could intercede on her behalf with that dictatorial son of hers, couldn't she?

Clinging on to that hope, Cathy glanced at her watch. Just an hour before she was due to meet up with Dona Luisa and, presumably, Javier. She shivered. She didn't know why, but she was beginning to tense up again. The Jerezano had an unfortunate effect on her. He had done, right from the start, and the way she'd mindlessly responded to his calculated caresses hadn't helped matters at all.

She could cope with his cold-blooded proposal of

marriage, because such a union was completely out of the question. But the memories of the way he had made her feel—like a sensual wanton—were something else again. They came back to haunt her at the most unexpected moments, made her go giddy. With shame, of course.

Her stomach was tying itself in knots as she flung open the door of the hanging cupboard. Rosa had unpacked for her earlier, and her few belongings looked pathetic and lost in the capacious depths. Dragging out the little black dress as being the most suitable garment she owned, she selected clean underwear and stamped through to the marble *en-suite* bathroom to shower, and was ready far too early.

Which gave her time to take proper stock of her surroundings, and that was preferable to trying to take stock of her situation, and about one hundred per cent better than contemplating seeing Javier again over dinner.

She had been given a beautiful room, she had to admit. Four tall windows overlooked what appeared to be extensive gardens, and the brocade wall-hangings in silver and sea-green took her breath away, the shimmering colours reflecting softly in the magnificent carved cedarwood ceiling. The glossy wood furniture was obviously antique and the chased silver bowls of white roses scented the air, and she could have been wonderfully happy while she was here if it weren't for Javier's dark demands, his terrifying threats.

Thankfully, for her peace of mind, Maria came, tapping on the door and beckoning, obviously intent on showing her to the *sala*, and that room was glorious, too: frescos and an elaborate, richly painted plasterwork ceiling. And, with a pang of something that should have been relief but which didn't really feel like it, she realised there was no sign of Javier.

'Now tell me. . .' Dona Luisa smiled over the rim of her second glass of *fino*. 'Did you enjoy yourself at the *finca*? I rarely go there these days, but I would have been there when you and Juan arrived if Javier hadn't told me you needed time to get adjusted to a new country, a new situation.'

That wasn't the way he had told it, Cathy fumed. Oh, how devious he was! Also, he had obviously made it sound as if she had come here for the duration. Well, his mother would have to be disabused. Gently. She couldn't be allowed to go on thinking that her grandson was to be a permanent fixture in her life. And Cathy was searching for a tactful way to explain all that when the older woman took her breath away, telling her, 'As Javier won't be able to join us this evening—some unavoidable business dinner, apparently—you and I can get to know one another. I simply can't tell you how pleased I am at his news. He had always said he would never re-marry—and he never says things he doesn't mean. It must have been fated. And entirely the best thing for dear little Juan.'

Was Dona Luisa saying what she thought she was saying? Cathy could hardly believe her ears. The rat! The sneaky, rotten rat! No wonder he had a pressing dinner engagement elsewhere! He must have told his mother that they were to be married. So that was why the older woman was already treating her as one of the family!

Obviously mistaking her flush of fury for one of girlish embarrassment, Dona Luisa laid her glass aside and patted Cathy's hand.

'You mustn't blame yourself for what happened with Francisco, my dear. He was an utter charmer and I am not yet so old that I cannot remember the fire and passion of youth. And things are different now from my younger days. Mistakes are not held against people for the rest of their lives. Society is far more tolerant. Not that Juan could be classed as a mistake,' she said quickly, with glowing sincerity. 'He is adorable. A blessing. And fate couldn't have dealt a kinder stroke than bringing you and Javier together.'

Cathy swallowed her sherry quickly. Someone was going to have to shatter this pleasant woman's rosy dreams. And it wasn't going to be her. Javier could do it, all by himself. It would be a just punishment, teach him not to tell lies! And she tried to put an interested look on her face when she and Dona Luisa went through to dinner and she was told, 'The Campuzanos, as a family, have not produced many sons. But the lack there they made up for by sheer astuteness. What sons they did have made good marriages. And they diversi-fied—wheat, olives, foreign investments and, recently, hotels in many parts of the world. You see, my dear——' she smoothed her linen napkin over her silk lap '—many of the old sherry families are no longer wealthy. What the vine disease—back in the early years of this century—didn't take, the war did. Now large international conglomerates own a great many of the *bodegas*, leaving many of the former sherry families with high heads but no wealth. Not so with the Campuzanos, I am happy to say. And Javier is building on our tradition of diversification in a big way, while always careful to ensure the success of our vineyards and *bodegas*.'

Bully for him, Cathy thought acidly. It was just a pity that all those fine old traditions hadn't taught him a thing about moral honesty and basic humility. Marry him, indeed! Stay where she was told to stay and fade into the wallpaper, hand over the baby to be brought up as he deemed fit, live the life of a nun and be thankful they weren't back in the days of the Inquisition!

None of this was allowed to show, of course. And her face was stiff with having to smile when she felt more like screaming, and her head ached with having to manufacture all those interested comments when she would far rather have been plotting suitable tortures for the infuriating Jerezano! And she said her warm goodnights to her would-be mother-in-law and went to bed feeling furious, and woke feeling bleak.

She could kiss goodbye to her hope of telling Dona Luisa the truth and enlisting not only her sympathy, but her help in dealing with Javier's impossible demands and definitely unidle threats. Juan's Spanish granny was over the moon at the prosect of a marriage that would keep them all one happy family with the 'blessing' of a grandson as a permanent reminder of the beloved son she had lost. So she wouldn't be feeling in a helpful frame of mind when she discovered that all her happy hopes were to remain unfulfilled!

'Why don't you go and get some fresh air and your breakfast?' Rosa asked, straightening up to wipe the bath-water off her face with the back of her hand. 'You look as if you didn't sleep too well.'

The two of them had put Juan in the big bath this morning, and he was loving every minute of the new adventure, sending cascades of water over both of them. Cathy scooped him out, wrapping his squirming body in a big white towel, and Rosa persisted, 'I can feed him and then take him out in the courtyard for his fresh air before the sun gets too hot.'

It wasn't a bad idea, Cathy was forced to admit. The baby would be in good and loving hands, and she needed to work out exactly what she'd say to Javier when next they met. That she would castigate him for telling lies to his poor deluded mother went without saying. But should she tell him outright thanks for the offer of marriage, but no, thanks, and risk what he might do in the way of legally prising the baby from her? Or should she carry on with the distasteful pretence of thinking his hateful proposal over?

Breakfast was the last thing on her mind, and she decided to make her way to the courtyard and sit and think while she waited for Rosa to bring Juan down for his airing. But she found herself in the garden, beneath her bedroom windows, found her feet taking her along a paved path, bordered by sweet-smelling carnations, to a curve of green grass punctuated by eucalyptus trees, their white trunks and silver leaves ghostly in the early morning mist.

She didn't know what she was going to do. After her father's defection her mother had leaned on her, forcing her to make decisions. And when, much to her private amazement, Cordy had decided to go through with having her baby it had been up to her to sort everything out. She had had to decide that, since Cordy obviously had to put her modelling career into cold storage for the time being, they should give up their separate and modestly affluent apartments and join forces in the much less salubrious north London flat. With only one of them earning, it was the best they could afford.

Cordy had complained, naturally, but Cathy had insisted that it was the only practical arrangement, for, despite her sister's confidence, she hadn't been at all sure that the coming baby's Spanish father would accept his responsibilities and, at the very least, provide handsomely for his child.

And one of the bravest yet, strangely enough, the easiest decisons she had had to make had been when the disillusioned Cordy had told her she could have the tiny child, that she could look after it, since she thought it the most perfect being ever created! She, Cordy, had had a job offer in the States, doing TV commercials for

a brand of soft drinks. No way was she going to pass
that opportunity up in order to stay home and change
nappies. Francisco Campuzano didn't care if he had
fathered a son, so why should she? Besides, she knew
someone who knew someone in Hollywood who could
wangle her a screen test.

So deciding, just like that, to give up her permanent
job and go freelance, to go for adoption with Cordy's
unreserved approval, had been easy.

Deciding what tack to take with the Jerezano was
not.

She shivered, wrapping her arms around her body,
and behind her came the sexy, unmistakable tones of
the man who was driving her quietly insane.

'Daydreaming, Cathy?' His hands were on her
shoulders and she went very, very still. In the cool,
misty morning she could feel his body heat as he stood
behind her, much too close.

Her throat went tight, but that didn't signify, because
she hadn't yet figured out how to handle him and the
situation he had created. A dignified silence was better
than a jumble of careless words. She made to move
away, but his grip tightened, swinging her round. And
the hard grey eyes beneath those straight black brows
swept her troubled face, the sensual mouth just slightly
amused as he told her, 'We will spend the day together
and I will show you something of my city. One day it
will be your city, too. I would like to be the one to
introduce you to it.'

'No.' It was very easy to refuse, and the word came
out on a definite snap. Dressed in a crisp white shirt
tucked into wickedly fitting black trousers, he pre-
sented a figure that would give the most sober female
alive naughty thoughts, and this particular sober female
had already had a lesson that had taught her all the
ungracious arts of self-defence.

'I insist.'

His voice was almost a purr, but there were slithers of flint in his beautiful eyes, and she found herself qualifying acidly, 'I have a baby to look after. But, of course, you'd quite forgotten.'

She watched him smile. It was the smile of a great predatory cat. And she wondered why until he said, 'Forgive me if I neglected you last night. My dinner engagement was unavoidable. But I do not intend to neglect you today. When I visited the nursery just now I instructed Rosa to look after Juan until we return—which she is delighted to do—and I relieved him of his wind.' His eyes crinkled unfairly, making her stupid heart miss a beat. 'I am getting expert at that, I think. I also taught him to say Papa.'

Which settled her silly heart quite nicely. Lying hound! He would, she was rapidly discovering, lie to anyone about anything, if it suited his devious purpose.

So yes, she would go with him, if only for a short while. Just long enough to tell him exactly how low liars came in her estimation!

Squashing the decidedly uncomfortable thought that she had done nothing but lie to him about her relationship to his nephew, she dragged in a deep breath, unaware of the way the action pushed her firm round breasts against the fine cotton of her sleeveless blouse, and opened her mouth to tell him that she would spend a couple of hours touring the town with him, when he cut her short, his eyes falling from her parted lips to her tilting breasts, his voice smoky and low as he said again, 'I insist, my dear. And in thirty-five years of living I have yet to meet the woman who can refuse. I will not believe that you are any different.'

CHAPTER SIX

CATHY knew she should be well used to his particular brand of arrogance by now, but it still took her breath away. And, aggravatingly, a retrospective flush stained her skin as she wondered if he had been slyly referring to the way she had allowed him to undress her, allowed him to play with her as good as naked body. If he had 'insisted' on ignoring her suddenly shamed protests, out there on the *campos*, 'insisted' on taking his lovemaking several steps further, would she have been able to deny him? Deny herself?

Of course not! The honesty of the answer made her legs feel hollow, and she swayed, stumbling against him.

'Steady.' His hand moved instinctively to help her, sliding for one tormenting moment around her waist, making her heart patter erratically against her breastbone.

And just for that one long moment their eyes held. His were eyes she could drown in, she thought bemusedly, and if he had been any other man she would have said he was as physically affected as she by the sudden body contact. But she knew better than that, didn't she?

Slowly, she dragged her eyes from his and allowed them to drift down to that sensually carved, utterly beautiful male mouth. She could almost feel it covering hers, tasting her lips, her tongue. . . Delving, devouring, possessing, caressing. . .

Cathy made a strangled sound in her throat. Oh, this was awful! How could she feel like this about him?

How could she want him so? Javier Campuzano, of all people! He was the very last man she should allow to get close. And he was, she admitted, beginning to panic, the only man to affect her this way. Ever. Even when she'd believed herself in love with Donald she had never looked at him and known this terrifying, overpowering urge to jump into bed with him, to have his naked body beside her, over her, within her. . .

'Don't pass out on me. We'll go to this place I know of for breakfast.'

There was an odd, rough edge to his voice, one she had never detected before. Or was it simply her imagination? Cathy didn't know. But she suddenly felt cold all over, knew her eyes were far too big for her face. Facing her own untenable feelings for him had been a blow. Shock did funny things to people. She circled her lips with the tip of her tongue, and Javier said with quick dark forcefulness, 'Let's go,' and took her arm in a biting grip, hurrying her over the precisely laid cobbles.

Because of her rampaging thoughts she hadn't realised they were in the deeply shaded narrow street, that Javier had closed the massive double door behind them, that she was alone with him again, away from the consoling proximity of Juan and Rosa.

She felt horribly vulnerable, wanting nothing more but to scurry back to the house. But she had to take this opportunity to get a few things straightened out: him telling his mother he had lied about their future relationship was one of them.

Stiffening her spine, she kept pace with him, looking around her to block out the beginnings of panic. The houses on either side of the street soared high above them, all with the iron *rejas* guarding the lower windows, all with the delicate tracery of ironwork around the upper balconies, all of them painted with that

lovely deep jade colour that went so well with the
golden stone of the buildings. And then they emerged
into the shimmering heat of a quiet square, set with
stone benches, shaded by palm trees, and perfumed by
orange trees.

Shakily, Cathy dragged in a deep breath and slowed
down, prising his fingers from her arm. His hand on
the bare flesh of her arm was, as far as he was
concerned, a mere courtesy. But she couldn't think
properly when he touched her, no matter how imper-
sonally. And she wanted to think, to observe.

'Well?' Straight black brows lowered as he halted
too, the grey eyes impatient, and Cathy's chin came
up. His mind might be on his breakfast, but she had
needs, too. And it was high time she made them
known.

'I made notes and sketches around the *finca*,' she
explained. 'For the paintings I shall do when I get
home to London. I intend to do the same here in
Jerez.' She extended a suddenly decisive hand. 'What
is this place? The architecture. . .'

She broke off, unable to find the words to convey
her delights, and Javier supplied with a snap,

'*Plaza del Progreso*. And that——' he gestured with
a long tanned hand '—the old Cabildo Municipal—
town hall, to you—built, I believe, in the late sixteenth
century. And there——' another terse hand movement,
telling her that his former irritation had turned into
anger '—the church of San Dionisio, named for our
city's patron saint. The architecture, if you are truly
interested, is Hispano-Arabic—known as *Mudéjar*—
and typical of Jerez.' The impatiently gesturing hand
snapped around her wrist. 'Enough of the travelogue.
You will have plenty of time to observe and take notes,
I promise.' And he set off at a pace that forced her to
trot, glad that she had chosen to team her cool white

blouse with a full black and white spotted cotton skirt and flat sandals. Otherwise, the pace he was setting as they skirted the massive church—all crumbling and magnificent in yellow stone, with plant life clinging tenaciously to cracks in the walls, and time-eroded, fissured gargoyles—would have had her falling over her own feet.

She was breathless as they emerged into another peaceful square on the other side of San Dionisio. The elegance of the central marble fountain, ornate street-lamps and wrought-iron seats were an intriguing contrast to the church's sturdy façade. And she knew then that she was beginning to be totally bewitched by the magic of this city, of Andalusia itself, all her annoyance, her mistrust of Javier, momentarily forgotten as her wide, glowing eyes met his and she breathed, 'I love it! I just love it!'

The taped, haunting voices of *cante jondo* singers coming from one of the bars made her heart flip over with a sudden, joyous sense of freedom, none of her cares and worries seeming to matter at all as his big body turned towards her, his hand sliding from her waist to capture her fingers, his warm grey eyes smiling into hers as they stood, encapsulated in the shimmering sunlight, the scent of orange blossom and the evocative music, oblivious of the sauntering passers-by.

'Then stay,' he commanded, his voice dark velvet. 'Don't talk to me about going back to London when we both know it isn't going to happen.'

And all the magic went, swept away by a harsh reality that wasn't magical at all.

He wanted her to stay, but locked in the cage of a nominal marriage, and only because his attempts to buy her off, bribe her into giving him all rights over his nephew, had failed. He had offered marriage—and in name only, she reminded herself bleakly—only as a final resort. And he expected her to accept. And even if she wanted to—which of course she didn't—she couldn't. Because if she were ever to be so unwise he would learn the truth about her relationship to little Juan, and she would lose the baby. This arrogant Jerezano, with the expert help of a team of hand-picked, expensive lawyers, would see to that.

Her face felt like stone and she watched his eyes narrow as his warm fingers released hers. And his voice was unamused as he deduced, 'So you are not yet willing to give me your acceptance. I'll let it go, for the moment.' His mouth went hard. 'But don't try my patience too severely, *señorita*. Come.'

And now was the moment to tell him how she felt about him: arrogant, heartless, the type of a man who would lie to his own mother. But she was too depressed now to think of starting on him, and spinelessly allowed him to seat her at a table outside one of the busy bars.

'You are hungry?'

Her eyes lifted reluctantly to lock with his. He had chosen a table beneath the shade of the trees, and the filter of green made his eyes look black. What was it about this man that made him immune to the feelings of others, so arrogantly sure that he would get what he wanted simply because he wanted it?

And why was she so perversely attracted to him? Was she unfortunate enough only to be attracted by a man whose need for total mastery was coloured and shaped by a streak of cruelty that could be disguised, at will, by the ability to charm?

Heaven help her, she thought bleakly. And shook her head. She couldn't eat a thing.

Which earned her a soft hiss of annoyance before he turned, snapping his fingers at a white-coated, liquid-eyed waiter who approached at once, beaming.

He seemed to be well known here, she thought. And

she could have slapped the smilingly deferential waiter for pandering to his already over-massive ego as his order of orange juice, coffee and lightly toasted rolls were produced in what had to be record time.

Her shadowed eyes on his long, lean fingers as he dribbled olive oil over his roll, she took a sip of her deliciously cold, freshly squeezed juice and reluctantly faced the fact that she couldn't go on hiding her head in the sand, like a silly ostrich, hoping Javier plus his terrifying insistence on marriage would go away.

Clearly, that was not about to happen.

Already his anger over her refusal to give him a decision was becoming alarmingly apparent, and somehow she had to find a way to make him see that the whole idea was crazy.

Edgily sipping at her *café solo* now, she cast around for some topic innocuous enough to use as a starter, because, despite his assurance that he would let the vexed question of his proposal go for the time being, those grey eyes were still coldly unforgiving beneath the lowered black bar of his brows.

So she offered inanely, her eyes on the golden globes of fruit among the green leaves above, 'It's strange, isn't it, how the orange tree flowers and fruits at the same time?' then wished she'd hadn't opened her mouth when he grated,

'Just like the woman who inhabits every young man's dreams—promise and fulfilment at one and the same time. But, unlike the tree, such a woman is sheer fantasy, belonging only in dreams.' His voice was harsh and his eyes were cold enough to turn the blood in her veins to ice. She couldn't imagine why such a neutral comment should have produced such a chilling reaction, and her hopes of starting a light conversation had been definitely put out of play. So she might as well forget her rather cowardly desire to get him in a pleasanter, more receptive mood, and wade straight in, get it over and done with.

'About your proposal. . .' she bit the bullet, her violet eyes unconsciously defiant as his brows rose beneath a slanting look that could only be described as suddenly complacent. 'It's not on. I've given it a lot of thought,' she said quickly, refusing to quail beneath the icy stare that followed so quickly on the heels of a fleeting flicker of blank disbelief. 'It would be a terrible mistake for all of us. You, me — and Juan.'

There, she had said it. And now all she had to do was make him admit that his idea had been hopeless. Somehow she had to placate his sinful pride, get him to agree with her and abandon his threats to rush off to the courts, surrounded by the top lawyers his vast wealth could command.

It wasn't impossible, surely? A shade unlikely — but not impossible. And when he leaned back in his chair, his fingertips pressed judicially together, his voice far too smooth as he questioned, 'Why? I would be very interested to hear how you arrived at such an amazing conclusion,' she felt distinctly queasy.

He was making a pretence at a willingness to listen to what she had to say, and to accord it his proper consideration. But he didn't fool her; she was beginning to know him too well. He was humouring her, as he would humour a child, having no intention of changing his mind.

Well, she wasn't a child and what she had to say to him made sense. A whole lot of sense. Determined to make him see that it did, hoping she sounded both rational and very sure of herself, she stated firmly, 'Your belief that our marriage would be in Juan's best interests doesn't hold water. If it ended in divorce it would have a terrible effect on him. His loyalties would be divided; you must see that. It would be much better for him in the long run if he were brought up by a single parent — me,' she injected quickly, so that there could be no mistake, 'knowing that whatever happened I would always be there, a constant in his young life.'

'There would be no divorce.' He sounded almost bored. 'So the question of divided loyalties wouldn't arise.' He put down a note to cover the bill, his eyes never leaving her face. 'If you've no further arguments to put forward, then I suggest we leave.'

She had plenty. She had hardly begun, and she told him as much, doggedly refusing to leave her seat even though he stood over her, looming and louring, the bite of his mouth living proof of the way she was trying his patience to the limit.

'Then I'm afraid they will have to wait; I was expected at the *bodega* half an hour ago,' he said coolly, making her hate him. And the now familiar click of his fingers, his 'Come', had her itching to slap his face. 'We will talk later,' he told her with infuriating smoothness as she shot to her feet in a temper, the glint in his eyes telling her quite clearly that he recognised her impotent fury and was slightly, insultingly, amused by it.

Cathy was tempted to refuse to go with him. Anywhere. To head straight back to the town house and start packing. But that wouldn't get her anywhere, would it?

And besides, although it had nothing to do with common sense, she wanted to be with him. Which wasn't completely crazy because he'd said they could talk after he'd taken her round the *bodega*, she assured herself as they left the narrow streets of the old quarter behind and crossed a wider thoroughfare where the flow of traffic was wild, the heavier vehicles threaded through with hordes of buzzing Vespinos, mostly ridden by youngsters with not a crash hat in sight.

But Javier gave her no time to comment, even if she'd wanted to. He marched arrogantly ahead, stepping aside for no one and nothing. He was still in a foul mood, she thought crossly, put there by her refusal to accept this proposal of marriage with cries of gratitude while falling to her knees and licking his shiny, hand-made shoes!

She was still trying to decide which kind of torture would give her the most pleasure to inflict on him when he marched down a relatively quiet street which appeared to be flanked on either side with nothing more exciting than warehouses.

Feeling hot and evil-minded, she followed and gave him barely a glance as he ushered her beneath an archway in a long white-painted wall. And before she had time to take in any details of the huge courtyard she found herself in, apart from the blaze of bougain-villaea tumbling over the inner walls, he was steering her through another archway, obviously in no mood to satisfy her curiosity.

Immediately, Cathy felt a hundred per cent cooler, and the contrast between the vibrant light outside and the dimness within disorientated her, sent her blundering into a group of people, grunting her apologies, before she finally cottoned on to what was happening.

They appeared to have caught up with a scheduled tour of the *bodega*, and Javier was handing her over to the guide, thankful to be rid of his excess baggage. No wonder he'd been in such an almighty hurry to get here. If they'd missed the start of the tour he might have felt obliged to show her round himself!

So much for his silky promise to show her around and explain the business of producing sherry.

Her eyes had adjusted to the interior gloom by the time Javier strode away from the group of tourists. And she watched him, noting the long-legged stride,

the forceful width of his shoulders, her eyes seething
with resentment. He had said he would spend the day
with her, and because she wouldn't agree to become
his wife he had dumped her at the first opportunity.
She could just imagine what married life with him
would be: do as you're told — or else!

But she hadn't agreed to spend the day with him out
of a desire for his fascinating company, she reminded
herself. She had seen it as the ideal opportunity to put
him right over his insulting proposal of marriage and
the sneaky way he had lied to his mother. So why
should she care if he off-loaded her?

Out of sorts with him and with herself, she scarcely
heard a word of what the guide was saying, although,
judging from the rapt expressions on the faces of her
companions, it was riveting. She would have much
preferred to wander away on her own, to savour the
almost cathedral-like atmosphere while she tried to get
her muddled emotions in order.

Already the cool, dark quietness was beginning to
soothe her troubled spirits and the smell of wood and
wine and moisture was balm to her agitated senses.

On either side of the coolly paved pathway underfoot
great oak butts rose, stacked in tiers almost to the high,
vaulted ceiling, the thickness of the walls keeping the
temperature down. And she had to give herself a sharp
mental shake when she found her feeble mind deciding
that she would have enjoyed having Javier at her side,
just the two of them alone in this cool, atmospheric
place while he explained everything to her.

She would have hated it, she informed herself tartly.
He wouldn't have been explaining a thing — except
exactly how he intended to take her baby from her
unless she did precisely as she was told.

'There are no vintage years in sherry,' the guide was
telling them. 'The use of the *solera* system ensures a

consistent quality—based on the fact that old wine is refreshed by the addition of a young wine, which, in turn, acquires the characteristics of the old one. It is a traditional form of blending.'

Cathy, forcing her mind away from the multitude of problems posed by the owner of these *bodegas*, began to concentrate, following the guide from one enormous cool *bodega*, or warehouse, to another, trying to absorb everything he told the group and failing dismally, she realised, as they were ushered into a huge building full of machinery which, as he told them, having to shout above the din, was the bottling plant.

The technicalities of sherry production were way over her head, although, she had to admit, she would have liked to learn a lot more about it. With Javier as tutor? her mind enquired wickedly, but she quickly blanked that thought out, mounting the metal steps with the rest of the group to a kind of observation platform.

'We'll be going to the tasting-room next,' one of the group shouted to another over the hissing and clanking, the rattle of glass against glass on the enormous conveyor belt, and Cathy smiled, deciding she was probably already intoxicated by the fumes, then felt her heart miss a beat as Javier walked over the plant floor beneath them and launched into an intense consultation with one of the workmen.

Unbelievably, she found herself longing to run down the metal steps, run across the concrete floor to where he stood. To claim him? To have him claim her, slide an arm around her waist, and draw her close against that vitally male body?

Shocked by her uncontrollable thoughts, she closed her eyes, refusing to allow the sight of those rangy white-clad shoulders, that shapely glossy dark head, to feed her stupid fancies.

What was wrong with her? How could she be so physically attracted to a man such as Javier Campuzano? He was her enemy; he was ruthless, devious and cruel. To be attracted to him was madness. Especially, she reminded herself sternly, since he had made it plain that he had no interest in her physically, that the marriage he was pressing for would be in name only. And the sexual advances he had made before had been nothing more than a chore for him, an attempt — abortive, as it had turned out — to seduce her and then triumphantly assert that such a promiscuous madam was no fit and proper parent for his nephew. It would have been just the proof he needed to add to the scurrilous snippets of information he had gleaned when he'd made enquiries into Cordy's reputation.

'Are you all right?' A motherly member of the group tentatively touched her shoulder and Cathy wrenched her eyes open, feeling a fool, and assured quickly,

'Yes, I'm fine, thank you. It's just so impossibly noisy.'

But she was far from all right, she decided miserably. With her eyes open again she could see that Javier had disappeared. Fool! she berated herself, wishing she could get back on her formerly even keel. She had closed her eyes to block out the sight of him and now that he was nowhere to be seen she felt devastated!

'Time for lunch.' She didn't need to turn around to know who was addressing her. She would recognise that sexy voice anywhere, and the light touch on her arm — to gain her attention, presumably — sent her pulses skittering out of control and, for a moment, she was giddy with relief. So he hadn't just dumped her, prepared to forget all about her and leave her to find her own way home.

But he mustn't even guess at her pathetic relief, she decided, ashamed of her feeble reactions. So she forced herself to take time over turning to face him, made her voice nice and cool as she objected, 'But the tour's not over yet. We still have to visit the tasting-room, I believe. And someone said something about casks that have been dedicated to famous personalities, and signed by them, and——'

'And I'll give you a personally conducted tour of the whole operation at some future date,' he injected tersely. 'I've just endured a long and tiresome phone conversation with our shippers in Cádiz. I need my lunch, even if you don't.'

There were small lines of strain around his eyes and mouth and, Cathy decided, he probably richly deserved them, then asked herself why, as she capitulated and turned to descend from the platform with him, she should suddenly feel uplifted, light as air, as she saw those tiny betrayals of inner tension disappear.

Nothing to do with her, of course. The brute needed feeding, not further hassle, and, having got his own way yet again, he was at ease with his world.

Emerging into the narrow streets from the coolness of the *bodega* was like walking into an oven, but even out here the scent of the living, breathing sherry was strong, so evocative of this richly unique and productive corner of Andalusia.

The brilliance of the light after the dimness hurt her eyes, and he must have noticed, because before she realised what was happening Javier turned her in through a narrow shop doorway, and before her eyes had a chance to readjust to the shady interior he had made his selection from a rack of sunglasses.

'Wear these.' He was sliding them on to her neat nose almost before she had realised he'd made the purchase. Cathy held her breath, fighting to hide the betraying tremors that shot all over her poor confused body whenever he laid a finger on her.

'They suit you.' He took a pace back, his head tilted to one side, appraising her. The corners of his mouth lifted. 'You have a lovely face.' His slightly hooded eyes drifted downwards. 'And that goes for the rest of you, too.' Which flustered her unbearably, making her head for the door, her shoulders stiff.

'You don't like compliments?' He caught up with her as she stamped down the hot pavement. He sounded mildly amused, and that annoyed her because she knew he knew she was over-reacting in a way that was almost juvenile.

If she had really been Juan's mother, Cordy, she would have lapped such compliments up, believing them to be her right. But for the life of her she couldn't put herself into the beautiful model's sophisticated character, and had to content herself with, 'No. Not unless they are sincere.'

'And why should you think they are not?' he wanted to know, a soft thrum of laughter making his dark voice sexier than ever as he took her arm, slowing down her headlong trot to a stroll. 'I would have thought, in your profession, you would deem such compliments commonplace. And as for sincerity, why should you think my reactions to a beautiful face and body would be any different from all other men's?'

Because I am not Cordy, and I am not beautiful, she answered inside her head. And you've already told me that even if we were man and wife you wouldn't want to lay a finger on me. And she was almost insanely relieved when he guided her into a bar which was almost like a *bodega*. Casks lined the walls, and there didn't seem to be a single tourist among the patrons, and the huge selection of *tapas* looked appetising enough to remind Cathy that she had been too uptight to eat any breakfast.

'Allow me to choose for you,' Javier suggested in his

normal dictatorial way, which made it not a suggestion at all, but an order. And Cathy, for once, was content to let it rest, allowing him to seat her at one of the few vacant tables.

'This is the very best way of sampling our wine and our food,' he commented as Cathy found herself looking at all those small dishes of various foods and a half-bottle of *fino*. 'To sip and sample will allow you to discover the happy knack our sherry has of complementing so many different types of food. Sherry, *tapas* and good conversation is the Jerezanos' favourite way of passing an hour or so.' He poured the pale wine into two glasses and leaned back, smiling into her eyes. 'So help yourself, and, to start the conversation rolling, tell me a little about yourself.'

'I thought you knew all there was to know from your former enquiries,' she returned, proud of her assumed nonchalance as she forked up a morsel of a delicously crisp shrimp fritter and followed it with a sip of *fino*. She didn't trust this new relaxed mood, nor his interest. He was easier to handle, on the whole, when he was bad-tempered, because now the temptation to go with the flow, relax and be her normal open self with him was severe. And dangerous.

'I mistakenly believed I did,' he acknowledged, his smile so warm that it turned her heart over. 'However, you puzzle me. Many things about you do not fit my preconceptions.'

Big of him to admit to any hint of that he could have been wrong about anything, she thought sarcastically, but swallowed the comment along with another sip of the delicate wine. Danger loomed. If he began to place his misconceptions together he might wander into a line of thinking that could bring him near to the truth.

'What's in that dish?' she asked, her voice high and brittle, and he obligingly pushed it over the table towards her with the tip of a long forefinger, his eyes all too knowing now, as if her reaction confirmed an idea he'd been turning over inside his handsome head.

'Stuffed artichokes. And don't neglect the classics.' More dishes slid her way. 'The ham, cheese and olives.'

She started talking about the food, asking him questions where she already knew answers. Why were the little dishes of food called *tapas* — literally translated as 'covers'? Because Spaniards didn't drink without eating, or rarely. The traditional slices of ham or cheese 'covered' the wine. All this she repeated to herself like a frantic litany, barely listening to his patient answers. She was trying hard not to panic, trying to assure herself that he wasn't getting near the truth, of course he wasn't, and had to fight hard to suppress a shriek of horror when he gave her a slow secret smile and announced silkily, 'If you've finished eating and babbling, we will find somewhere peaceful and shady to talk.' He rose, extending a hand that wasn't meant to be ignored. 'I want to hear all about your life, your background, your family. Everything. As your future husband, I insist. Come.'

CHAPTER SEVEN

FUTURE husband? Was he never going to get that vicious bee out of his bonnet? And why was he so sure that a real marriage, for all the right reasons—love, respect and the getting of an heir for himself—was impossible?

Had he loved his first wife so deeply that he couldn't and wouldn't replace her? Was that why he could so dispassionately consider naming his dead brother's son as his heir, taking the child's mother as his nominal wife because, since she couldn't be bribed to go away and stay away, she had become a disagreeable and immovable part of the package?

And what if he was beginning to guess the truth— that she wasn't the baby's mother at all? It didn't bear thinking about, and yet she couldn't dismiss the fear from her mind.

'Here, I think.' Javier stopped at an unoccupied wrought-iron seat beneath the shade of an immense palm, and Cathy sat down gratefully, worn out with worrying. Suddenly, she longed to be able to talk to Cordy, to discuss the way her life had been taken over since the handsome Jerezano had walked into her London flat. It was dreadful to have no one to share one's anxieties with, even though she could second guess what Cordy would say: let him have the kid; Johnny will be much better off in the long run.

Cathy frowned, twisting a little on the seat, trying not to look at Javier, who was angled into the corner of the bench, one arm along the back, completely relaxed, looking at her, the slight smile in his grey eyes

giving nothing away. Had she so suddenly thought of
Cordy, of what her advice would undoubtedly be,
because she knew it was the truth? Because she was
beginning to feel selfish and guilty? Juan—Johnny—as
Javier's heir would definitely have a better quality of
life here in Jerez. With the Campuzano wealth behind
him he would have the best of everything throughout
life. He would also have love, she acknowledged at
last. Javier doted on him, so did Dona Luisa, and
Rosa, she knew, would be his devoted slave as long as
she had breath in her young body. And, surrounded by
such loving care and devotion, the baby wouldn't miss
her. He wouldn't pine; he was far too young.

But she would miss him. She would pine. If she gave
him up there would always be an ache in her heart, an
ache in the arms that would never again hold him. Was
she being wickedly selfish?

Tears clogged her throat and she fixed her eyes on
the magnificent equestrian bronze that was the centre-
piece of the huge fountain in the middle of the square,
trying to concentrate on that and not on the unpalatable truth that had sliced into her mind with the sharp
pain of a rapier thrust.

The raised bronze was surrounded by dolphins and
angels and there were box-edged beds of sweet scented
phlox, snapdragons, roses and lilies. The sound of the
cooling spray from the fountain almost drowned out
the noise of the traffic on the narrow streets that
surrounded the square, and Javier commented lazily,
'You are very silent, *querida*.'

It was the first time he had used an endearment. Her
skin burned, even though she told herself it meant
nothing. Nothing at all. And she gave him a quick
empty smile, hoping she was disguising the pain the
idea of her own selfishness had brought, and the

miserable consequences for her, and said brittly, 'This is a truly beautiful square.'

'The Plaza del Arenal is the finest in Jerez,' he acknowledged, an arrested look in his eyes as he took in the details of her face, as if he were truly seeing her for the first time. 'The first public riding exhibition of high dressage was given here, back in the seventeenth century, and——'

'Has that anything to do with the shows that are put on here in Jerez?' she butted in quickly, thankful to be on neutral ground, because, the way she felt now, all over-emotional, she couldn't handle the probing questions he had threatened.

'You are talking of the Royal Andalusian School of Equestrian Art. You have heard of it?' he wanted to know, his glossy dark head tipped to one side, and she told him,

'Of course. Who hasn't?' Which earned her a grin of such charm and warmth that her poor heart went into top gear.

'Then I shall take you to watch how the Andalusian horses dance,' he promised softly. 'For Jerez, apart from being the city of sherry and flamenco, is the Spanish capital of the horse. Are your parents still alive? Does Juan have grandparents I do not know of, and should meet?'

The unwanted, abrupt change of subject had been thrown at her so unexpectedly—too unexpectedly. Cathy simply stared at him, feeling her body go rigid with tension. And she met the slow, frowning assessment of his eyes and knew he knew that, for a reason as yet unknown to him, it was something she didn't want to discuss.

But she could handle it. She had to handle it. Until she had had the opportunity to minutely examine her own conscience and decide whether or not hanging on for grim life to the baby she loved as if he were her own was the right thing to do, she had to keep him in ignorance of Cordy's existence.

So she said edgily, 'My mother died a few years back, but my father walked out ten years ago, when I was fifteen. All we knew was that he went to South America with another woman. He'd been having an affair with her for years, apparently, and Mother never knew. Wives are supposed to, aren't they? We never heard from him again.' And before he could start asking about brothers or sisters and force her to lie to him, yet again, she pumped herself up into a state of righteous anger, which wasn't too difficult when she remembered, and snapped, 'My family, or lack of one, isn't important. What is important is the question of our marriage. It's a ridiculous idea, and you know it.' From the corner of her eye she saw him stiffen, and refused to look at him, to endure all that Spanish pride, that anger.

She kept her eyes on the triple fountain instead, all those dancing, iridescent jets of water, and carried on firmly, 'You say there would be no question of a divorce, but what would happen if one of us fell in love?' As she could, all too easily, fall in love with him.

The self-knowledge was truly unpalatable, bringing an idiotic lump to her throat. She swallowed it. But her voice was more husky than she was comfortable with as she tried to explain, 'I might not want to live the life of a pampered nun. I might want a child. . .' She caught herself, hoping she hadn't given too much away, and altered rapidly, 'More children. I'm the maternal type.' And she was. The depth of her feelings for the baby Cordy hadn't wanted had surprised her. 'Besides, I dare say you think now that no other woman could ever take your first wife's place. But you might fall in love and want to marry her, to give her your children.

It's not inconceivable, after all. And then where would we be?'

The facts in a nutshell, she thought, too factual and logical for him to brush aside lightly. He wasn't an idiot. And she wondered why she felt so disconsolate, but only for a moment, because she knew the truth of it. She knew that if he loved her, which he didn't and never would, she would be the happiest female on the planet and would marry him tomorrow and let him sort Cordy out.

She didn't know what form his reaction would take and was speechless, incapable of any movement, when he got abruptly to his feet and strode away, never looking back, his broad-shouldered, lithely moving body melting into the shadows beyond the gaily playing fountains.

I could get used to this, Cathy thought dreamily. It was a rare moment of total relaxation at the end of a forty-eight-hour span that had had her nearing the limits of her sanity. She hadn't set eyes on Javier since he had walked away from the Plaza del Arenal—a suddenly important business trip, Dona Luisa had explained, a trace of embarrassed apology in her fine eyes. She had obviously had no liking for the role of go-between, passing messages between an engaged couple. Perhaps she was already having doubts about their supposed relationship. If so, it was all to the good. The truth, when she learned it, wouldn't come as such a blow.

Besides, she, Cathy, had just done what she should have done the moment Javier had put in an appearance back in London. She had written to Cordy, explaining everything.

So perhaps the slight easing of her conscience had contributed to this welcome feeling of relaxation. That, and the scented cool of the evening, the long windows

to the *sala* open behind her as she sat in the dusky
courtyard listening to the sleepy sound of doves, the
clear splash of the water as it trickled from the ornate
fountain into the stone basin beneath.

No use wishing now that she had taken the baby and
found another flat in another part of London when
Cordy had finally stopped hoping Francisco would
contact her. If she had, then Javier would not have
found them. But she couldn't have known he would
try, couldn't have known what the fates had in store—
that she was destined to lose her heart to the handsome
Jerezano and, in all probability, lose the baby she
adored.

She should never have lied. She should have told
him the truth about Cordy. Even if those lies had been
told for what she had believed to be the best of reasons,
he would add them up and hold them against her,
believing her to be as tainted as her sister, neither of
them fit to be entrusted with the care of his nephew.

He was ruthless and single-minded, but he wasn't
wicked. Had she been honest, right from the start, he
would have acknowledged the personal sacrifices she'd
made to keep the baby with her, understood her love
for the child. And they could have worked something
out between them. He would never have separated her
from Juan, had he believed in her integrity. She knew
that now. Too late.

Hindsight was useless. Cathy sighed, compressing
her soft lips against her teeth as the tension came
creeping back. And behind her Javier said softly, 'Why
so sad, Cathy *mío*?' and came to stand before her, his
dark-suited figure shadowy in the dusk, his features
hidden. 'If I am responsible for that deep, deep sigh,
then my apologies are even more necessary.' Gravely,
he handed her a glass of chilled *manzanilla* and sat

beside her, and Cathy's fingers trembled on the misty surface of the glass.

She hadn't known he was here, and his appearance seemed magical, as if her thoughts of him, the feelings she scarcely dared admit to, even in the tortured privacy of her own mind, had conjured his disruptive presence into the quiet peace of the scented evening. She shivered, not knowing how to handle the harried bundle of fears and yearnings, packaged in a wild welter of emotions she had never experienced before that made up her reaction to this man.

'You are cold? You would prefer to go inside?' He was sitting beside her now, and the faint glow of light from the *sala* illuminated dark features that were taut and strained.

Cathy shook her head, her long, pale hair falling forward to veil her face as she expelled the breath she hadn't realised she'd been holding. She couldn't have moved, even if she'd wanted to, and she told him thinly, 'Not cold. Just pleasantly cool. It's been sweltering today.'

'Good. I need to talk to you. Out here we may count on a little privacy before dinner.' He sounded weary, and fell to silence, and the silence stretched and her ears were straining to hear what he had to say to her, but no words came. And she knew that he had at last listened to reason, that what she'd had to say to him the last time they'd spoken had struck a chord of logic.

And, in the moment of his own choosing, he would tell her as much, would admit that his idea of marriage had been illogical, and that would hurt. Because, even though she'd known she could never marry him, not on his terms, his insistence on it had given her a queer, inverted sense of pleasure, although she would never have admitted to it at the time.

While he had still seen marriage as a tidy way around

the problem of custody of Juan he had kept his eye on her — sometimes distant, sometimes close, but always making her aware of it. And she needed his presence in her life, in any capacity, just as a junkie needed his fix. And she didn't know what she was going to do about it. She had grown used to his darkly brooding presence, to the passionate line of his mouth, to the fire in his eyes and the warm dark velvet of his voice. . .

'I want to apologise.' Finally he spoke, and she gave him a wary glance. He was sorry for having made the mistake of proposing, insisting? Contrition wasn't part of his make-up, as she knew it. His rare mistakes would be shrugged aside, marked down to experience and promptly forgotten. 'I'm sorry I walked away and left you,' he went on, throwing her preconceptions out of play. 'When you talked about my wife you caught me on the raw, reminded me of things I believed I had forgotten. But that was no excuse,' he said bleakly, 'for behaving as I did. I should have had more control.'

So she had been right, Cathy thought wretchedly. He had loved his wife so much that after her death he couldn't bear the thought of putting any other woman in her place, loved her so much that even hearing her mentioned was enough to make him lose all control.

He finished his own *manzanilla* and placed the glass carefully between them on the stone bench they shared. A barrier? Was he afraid she might try to move closer, to push her unwanted sympathy into the hallowed arena that was his memory of the woman he had loved beyond all else?

She felt about two inches high and knew she had to end this encounter while she still retained a little pride, so she swallowed the remainder of her drink and very precisely set her glass beside his, reinforcing the barrier if that was what he wanted, she thought brittly, and, doing her best to sound offhand, told him, 'Think nothing of it; I didn't. I enjoyed exploring the old city on my own and found my way back here with no trouble at all.' And she would have left him then, left him to brood over the lost love of his life, if that was what he needed, but his terse voice stopped her.

'I want to tell you about Elena. We don't need secrets. Which was one of the reasons I asked you about your family. Everything has to be out in the open if we are to share any kind of relationship.'

They weren't. After he had learned the truth he wouldn't want to have her round in any capacity at all. And it seemed inevitable that he would, sooner rather than later. Her hope that she would hear through Molly that her adoption request had gone through while she was here in Jerez had been stupidly impractical. Molly had warned her and she hadn't wanted to listen. Until the authorities were well and truly satisfied that Cordy wouldn't have a change of heart — and that could take months, if not years — then she wouldn't be able to adopt legally. And why, after all she had said on the subject, was he still talking in terms of relationships in any case?

But he was saying something to her and she had no option but to listen and as he spoke her eyes widened, in disbelief at what she was hearing at first, and then with compassion, because everything was quite different from what she had believed.

'When a Campuzano marries it is for one of several reasons,' his quiet voice was explaining. 'For position, for added wealth or land, for getting an heir. Passion, its fickle nature, does not figure on the list. But I——' his voice took on a note of self-disgust '—in my folly, acted differently from my forebears. Had my father still been alive he might well have brought pressure to bear, persuaded me to wait until we knew one another better.' The wide, rangy shoulders lifted expressively beneath the expensive suiting. 'But maybe not. My blood was hot and I knew what I wanted. Elena.' The word was like a wraith, drifting between them, and Cathy shivered and hoped he had not noticed, sensing the bleak residue of pain inside him although not properly understanding it. Not yet.

And after long moments while the evening darkened around them he spoke again, almost lightly now.

'She, too, was English. Unlike you, though, both her parents were very much around. She was an only child, born late to them, and she was a beauty. I can understand, though not condone, the way they spoiled her. Two or three months before I met her, her father had retired. He bought an apartment on Playa de Valdegrano, roughly halfway between here and Cádiz, and they settled here to enjoy the climate. Elena, of course, came with them. I first saw her during the *Fiestas de la Vendimia*—when the grape harvest is being blessed—and from that moment I was bewitched. I pursued her as if she were the last woman on earth. I wanted her until I thought I would go up in flame. She was just nineteen.' He leaned forward, his arms across his knees, tilting his head abruptly in her direction, and his tone was harsh as he asked, 'Can you understand such an obsession?'

She could. Oh, yes, she could. Hadn't it happened to her? Not quite so immediately, but quite as inevitably. Loving him, she knew the meaning of hopeless obsession.

'I think so,' she answered quietly, wincing a little at his grated,

'Well, I don't! *Cristo*, I was hardly a child! I was almost thirty, my father's son—astute, level-headed, almost too well balanced. And all it took was skin-deep beauty, bewitching eyes, teasing smiles, seductive promises and tantalising withdrawals to turn me into a mental and physical wreck. Nothing could prevent me marrying her and claiming all she had promised. The wedding was a sumptuous affair, one of the most splendid Jerez has seen. The celebrations lasted a week. But they were over for me as soon as the door to the bridal suite closed behind us.' His voice was splintered ice now, and Cathy held her breath. 'No sooner had she unpinned her veil than she began to lay down the ground rules, as she called them. I was not to make "unreasonable demands". She enjoyed flirting with men, but that was as far as it went. She had already had a few experiences of the aftermath of flirtation, but on each occasion had found the experience embarrassing, uncomfortable and messy. But she was willing to be fair; in exchange for the advantages of my position and wealth, she could be no less. I would be permitted to share her bed one night in each week until a child had been conceived. She drew the line at more than one, however. All this so coolly, so dispassionately. She was like a child pulling the legs from a beetle, not knowing of the pain she was inflicting.'

'Oh, how could she?' Cathy whispered, appalled, her voice barely audible against the fluid music of the fountain, the splash of the water as it sluiced into the stone basin.

Javier straightened, turning to find her eyes in the velvet night.

'Easily. What does a spoilt child do when it wants something? It grabs. Elena wanted wealth and she was just about adult enough to know how to bait the trap, how to use her beauty, how to make empty promises to get what she wanted. But she wasn't mature enough to figure out the consequences. The marriage was never consummated. She was truthful, at least, and her truth extinguished all that burning passion, as if it had never

been. And for two years we only met in the company
of others, although we shared the same house. She had
all the toys she'd craved, the clothes, jewels, horses,
foreign holidays. I never asked if she was happy. I
didn't care. For me she barely existed. The marriage
could have been annulled, of course, but I saw little
point. For one thing, I had too much pride and, for
another, I knew I would never marry again. I would
not make a fool of myself twice.'

'But all women are not like that,' Cathy reminded
him gently, understanding now why he had spoken so
bitterly when she had talked about the orange trees—
promise and fulfilment at the same time. Elena had
promised but had refused to deliver. And she sensed,
rather than saw, his dismissive shrug.

'You are probably right. But what of me? How could
I trust the fickle emotion again? I believed—I was so
sure—that I loved Elena more than my soul. Yet when
it came right down to it, it was nothing but lust, a
raging need for what she so cleverly denied. Had I
loved her, it would have overcome my pride. I would
have been patient, taught her—slowly and gently—
how truly incandescent the physical manifestation of
love can be. Not loving her, my pride took over and
allowed me, quite unemotionally, to disregard her. I
even gained an arid satisfaction from watching her
discard one toy for another, seeking something she
couldn't find. She was killed behind the wheel of the
last one she ever had,' he said sombrely. 'Now can you
understand why I can never again allow myself to
believe I can love?'

Compassion, mixed with a terrible need to take him
by the hand and patiently teach him that he, like every
other human being, was capable of love, welled inside
her, making her feel as if her heart would burst, and

she asked shakily, 'Did your family know how unhappy your marriage was?'

'I think my mother and the veritable army of ancient aunts I am blessed with guessed.' She glimpsed the quick white flash of his teeth in the darkness. 'But they knew me better than to ask. My mother had warned me about the almost indecent haste of the wedding; she thought Elena too immature for me. And Francisco was too busy being a young man and enjoying a young man's pleasures to give the state of my marriage more than a passing thought. Besides——' he shifted slightly, turning as if trying to read her expression in the soft, sweet darkness '—the word unhappy doesn't truly describe the state we found ourselves in. Elena found she had everything she wanted, materially, without having to endure the embarrassing discomfort of my presence in her bed for the grudgingly offered one night a week, and I certainly didn't wet my pillow with tears. My pride was hurt, but not my heart. I was angry because I had allowed myself to be used, made a fool of.'

'I'm sorry,' Cathy whispered, hurting for him. How terrible that he should believe himself incapable of love, unable to trust any emotion that he couldn't describe as lust. It made her heart weep just to think of it.

'I don't need your pity, or want it!' The sudden harsh savagery of his voice shocked her and she caught her breath, hating this return of cold anger. 'I wanted you to know. It will help you understand why our marriage will be one of convenience only.'

So he was back to that troublesome subject, was he? Cathy did the only thing she could. She got to her feet, desperately trying to smooth the sharp edges out of her voice as she told him, 'I'm sure Dona Luisa has already had to hold dinner back for us. And, talking about

your mother, you did a despicable thing when you lied
to her. Not even for Juan's sake am I willing to marry
you—I've already explained why. So you'd better put
her straight, hadn't you?'

She was already almost at the open *sala* windows,
her face flushed with angry colour, when he reached
her side and dropped an arm around her bristling
shoulders, and his voice was wickedly warm and dark
as he dipped his head and murmured against her ear,
'For that small sin I have no apology to make, *querida*.
By telling Mama of our plans I was forcing the issue—
since you seem so reluctant to face the inevitable. You
know how she already idolises the child and, from my
observations of you, I find you have a soft heart. You
couldn't disappoint her; you know you couldn't!
Besides——' that insulting trace of amusement was
back with a vengeance '—I didn't lie about our marriage. It is nothing short of the truth.'

All through dinner she was too angry to speak, too
angry to do more than push her food around with the
prongs of her fork. How dared he? How dared he put
her through all this? Did he think she was another
Elena, easily satisfied with material advantages? Did
he think she could risk losing her baby altogether when
he discovered the truth? And even if by some large
miracle he didn't find out she wasn't his nephew's
biological mother, did he think that she could endure
the sterile relationship he demanded, when she loved
him so much?

But he didn't know that, did he? she reminded
herself with a large, defeated sigh. And he mustn't ever
find out. If he did it would be the pits when it came to
the humiliation ratings. And, to be fair to him, he had
been honest with her from the start. Brutally so. It was
she who had repeatedly lied. She didn't know how she

was going to live with the consequences — or with herself, come to that.

'Cathy hasn't heard a word you've said.'

At the sound of her name she looked up and met his eyes. Warm eyes. But the warmth didn't hide the question in the clear grey depths, a question that had suddenly found an answer, she decided as a knowing amusement completely took its place.

Quickly she dropped her gaze, fixing it on the mangled food on her plate, and bit down hard on her bottom lip. Had he guessed her true feelings? Had he? Was she so transparent?

'Poor Cathy, you are tired,' Dona Luisa said sympathetically, and Cathy grabbed the lifeline, her smile an effort.

'I think I am, rather.'

'And I think you spend too much time out in the sun making your drawings. You should be firm with her, Javier,' the older woman teased. 'However, tomorrow I am taking charge — no dusty streets and burning sun. We are going shopping.'

'Are we?' It was the first she'd heard about it. But then Javier was, as ever, right. She hadn't been listening to the conversation.

'Something to do justice to your beauty, especially for the occasion. It will be my pleasure. I want to show you off — as Javier does, too, of course.'

Dona Luisa was practically rubbing her hands in anticipation, and Javier explained lightly, 'Mama is giving a reception for you tomorrow evening; we both want you to look your best.'

'Only the family, of course,' Dona Luisa assured her quickly, misinterpreting her sudden frown. 'We are still officially in mourning. You will meet all our friends later, I promise.'

'Simply the army of ancient aunts,' Javier put in

drily, leaning back in his chair, his grin unrepentant. 'However, the ordeal will be eased by a little food, a little wine and your first taste of flamenco.'

'Javier!' Dona Luisa tutted her disapproval, but, faced with his lazy good humour, dimpled, telling Cathy, 'My husband's sisters—all six of them—were all born before him. He was the last child, the only son. As I once told you, the Campuzanos do not sire many male children. And my brother, Antonio, is in Mexico. He has lived and worked there most of his adult life. So the aunts are all we have, and, despite what my reprobate son is trying to say, they are not in the least frightening.'

'I'm sure they're not,' Cathy agreed quickly. She wasn't going to be able to wriggle out of this, much as she would have liked to, and she supposed the little black dress that had been dutifully trotted out each evening was beginning to look both horribly familiar and not a little tired. 'But I can buy my own dress,' she stated, wondering if the emergency money she'd brought with her would run to anything fit to be seen in, and was quickly put in her place by the Jerezano, who stated in his most lordly tones yet, 'I do not doubt it. Nevertheless——' he gave his mother a warning look '—it will be my pleasure to pay for what you need. Not only something suitable for tomorrow evening, but more cool and casual clothes.' And again to his parent, who was nodding approvingly, 'I think Cathy was surprised by the strength of our Andalusian sun. I should have prepared her better. Therefore, her lack of enough suitable clothing is entirely my fault and it will be my pleasurable duty to put things right.'

Cathy could have spat in his eye! The last thing she wanted was his charity, and the last thing she wanted to acknowledge was the fact that he must have noticed the meagreness of her wardrobe.

But Dona Luisa was almost bouncing up and down in her chair, like a child with a favourite outing in the offing. And when she actually clapped her fine-boned hands together and twinkled, '*Olé!*' Cathy knew she had lost the battle before it had even begun.

CHAPTER EIGHT

'AH, *QUÉ GUAPA*! How pretty you look!' Rosa enthused as Cathy opened her bedroom door to the other girl's knock. 'The shopping was a great success, I can see that!'

Stepping aside for Rosa to enter, Cathy had to agree that it had been. Too successful. Apart from the floor-length sheath in silk that exactly matched her eyes and made even her voluptuous figure look elegant, she was now the uneasy possessor of an entire new wardrobe. Not content with the evening dress and a few cool casuals, Dona Luisa had bought up the contents of several exclusive boutiques—or so it had seemed.

Once she had started, she didn't know how to stop and, after a while, Cathy had given up fighting her and had let it all happen, enjoying the older woman's irrepressible enthusiasm.

But when she returned to England she would leave it all behind. There was no way she would take anything back with her that would remind her of Javier. It would be far too painful. Except the sketches, notes and photographs for the paintings she meant to execute. Apart from being her livelihood they would represent her tribute to a part of the world she was growing to love more with each passing day.

'Juan, he is asleep?' Rosa wanted to know, and Cathy nodded, cursing the lump that formed in her throat.

Soon she was going to have to tell Javier the truth; her conscience wouldn't allow her to continue with her lies. And she knew what would happen then. He would

120

fight for custody of his nephew with every weapon in his considerable armoury.

'Then I will sit with him, in case he wakes,' the Spanish girl promised. 'Today his cheeks were flushed — I think he might be teething again — and Don Javier asked me to tell you that the guests will be arriving soon; he asks you to hurry.'

Now she tells me! Cathy watched Rosa tiptoe into the adjoining nursery, a paperback in her hand, and turned to the mirror, suddenly nervous. She would be meeting all those aunts under false colours. She hoped to heaven that Dona Luisa hadn't told them that she and Javier were to be married!

She hadn't even thought about that possibility until now, and now that she had she wished she hadn't. If only Javier hadn't lied! If only she had told the truth in the first place then none of this could ever have happened!

But it was no use agonising over what couldn't be changed, she informed her wild-eyed reflection. She just had to get through the evening as best she could, and if her eyes were too glittery and her cheeks too flushed they could all put it down to excitement and feel pleased with themselves.

Despairingly, she wondered if her long hair, left loose, made her look like a matron aping a teenager. The single braid she normally affected had looked out of place with the sophistication of her new and horrendously expensive dress. And she had tried to put her hair up, she really had. But she didn't have the knack, and five seconds after she'd thought she'd secured it firmly it had all come tumbling down.

Compromising, she'd drawn two wings of hair back from her face and secured them with a clip she'd borrowed from Rosa earlier on, leaving the rest loose, flowing down her back. And it was going to have to

do, because there was no time to experiment again
with the more suitable upswept style.

Resisting the impulse to go back to the nursery to
check on Juan, delaying the start of an evening that
promised to be unadulterated embarrassment if Dona
Luisa had told all her sisters-in-law that Javier was to
marry the mother of Francisco's illegitimate son, Cathy
threw back her shoulders and left her room, and
discovered that all the guests had already arrived.

Expecting to see censure for her lateness in Javier's
stern grey eyes, her breath was taken away when she
encountered instead a look of intense approval. Admiration, really, she had to admit, feeling her flesh begin
to quiver beneath the warm, slow drift of his eyes as
they assessed every detail of her silk-clad body.

An admiration that was really nearer to open sexual
appraisal, she decided wildly as a flood of shattering
sensation was released inside her, making her skin
burn, her blood turn to fire in her veins. She was far,
far too aware of him, of the many facets of his
character, of his power over her—the power to make
her love him, the power to give her pain, and the fact
that his strength lay not only in his capacity for cruelty,
but in his infinite gentleness, too.

And the longer they were locked together in their
small and silent world of mutual private assessment,
the more she felt in danger of fragmenting into tiny,
irreparable pieces, and she tore her eyes from his with
an effort she felt must show and painted a tiny,
unknowingly uncertain smile on her face as she turned
to be introduced.

And promptly forgot every last one of their names.
But Javier was at her side to help her, the hand cupping
her elbow more proprietorial than merely courteous,
never leaving her, stuck like a limpet, making her
wonder if, for her, the evening would end in hysterics.

Because he was behaving like a lover, every glance, every whispered word of explanation or comment, an open caress, a nuance of adoration.

And he wasn't behaving this way because his mother had relayed his lies about their marriage. Not one of the ancient aunts, or the single ancient uncle, had mentioned it. They had mentioned everything else under the sun, or so it seemed, but not a forthcoming wedding. So nothing could have been said, which meant he wasn't playing a part to give outward veracity to his dark and dreadful lie.

And it wasn't because he was seeing her looking her best, dressed with elegance and style for once instead of in the usual well-washed, much worn garments that comprised her scanty wardrobe. He would have seen better.

A lavish buffet meal had been put out in the *sala*, and the aunts, their tongues eased by the delicious food and fine wine, bombarded her with questions in charmingly accented English, but kindly. What did she think of Spain? Of Jerez? Had she visited their wonderful clock museum in the Palacio de la Atalaya? Was it true that in England it always rained?

Only one of them mentioned the baby; the others were too polite, Cathy felt, as that large lady invited, 'You must bring the little one to visit me. Javier shall arrange it. Is it true that he resembles Francisco when he was that age?'

'Exactly, Tía Carlota, down to the last dimple, I believe,' Javier put in smoothly, at his most attentive, the ball of his thumb caressing the soft flesh of her inner elbow as the stout Carlota turned away to relay this snippet of information in contented undertones to one of her sisters.

Cathy shivered. The hidden intimacy of his touch made her bones feel as if they were about to disintegrate. Remembering the time when he had undressed her, stroked her willing body with sensual expertise, she shivered again. He had had an ulterior motive that time. He must have one now. Mustn't he?

'Don't let her worry you,' Javier murmured, his grip tightening just a little on her arm, misinterpreting those tiny tremors. 'Tía Carlota has a heart of pure gold. Only three of my aunts married, and as she is the only one with a surviving husband—Tío Emilio, who you now see being deferred to by the three unmarried aunts, which, in itself, has become quite a ritual—she has set herself up as leader of the pack.'

His quiet, dry humour calmed her and she accepted the glass of wine he gave her, thankful that the evening, so far, had not been anything like the ordeal she had imagined. And if he was being more than usually attentive, then she would try not to think anything of it. With all those old aunts around he was probably assuming the mantle of good behaviour to please his mother. She would not be suspicious.

At last there seemed to be a general, though, as far as Cathy could tell, unorchestrated movement out of the room, and Javier, close by her side still, told her lightly, 'We go to the *sala grande* where we are to be entertained by La Gitana, for your benefit. And do not think us too old-fashioned, *querida*.'

He eased her forward, the palm of his hand on the small of her back. An inch higher and he would encounter bare flesh where the silky fabric dipped with an elegance of line that made it appear less daring than it was. Cathy's skin tightened, as if in anticipation, every last one of her senses concentrated on the warmth of his hand through the silk, gritting her teeth as she waited for the inevitable—desired?—slide upwards that would bring skin to skin, flesh to flesh, barely comprehending him as he told her, 'This reception is small, of necessity, and only the aunts are old-fashioned. One day you will see how such things can be — glittering occasions, the cream of society, many young people, and after the entertainment, the dancing, the music. One day, I promise, you will see. I will give a ball for you that will be sumptuous beyond your wildest dreams.'

She could have answered that it was unlikely that she would be here that long, or that he would want to do her such honour when he learned the truth about her, the way she had deceived him right from the start. But she had neither the wit nor the desire. His hand had found the dip in her neckline and his fingers were lightly resting on the over-sensitised skin of her back. She was incapable of coherent speech. Her desire for him to touch her, really touch her, overwhelmed her.

But she could see what he'd meant when he guided her in through massive double doors and the *sala grande* lay before them in all its magnificence.

Hauling herself together, she moved away from him, trying to remove herself from his dangerous aura, out of the haze of sensuality that was blocking her senses to every last thing except his touch, his nearness, the soft warm velvet of his voice.

This was a room she had not discovered during her stay here, and she didn't need much imagination to see it as the perfect setting for a society ball, thronged with the beautiful, the wise, the witty and wealthy, a small orchestra playing on the raised dais at the far end, the tall windows marching down the impressive length of one wall opening on to the arcaded veranda that led down to the silent, secretive night-time gardens.

Smooth marble underfoot would make the perfect surface for dancing, and she wouldn't even dare to try to imagine what it would be like to be held close to Javier, swept along in his arms, drifting and dreaming beneath the glittering lamps high upon the carved and painted ceiling.

She moved quickly forward, high, slender heels tapping on the marble. The immense room had been partly partitioned, and there were ten gilded chairs in an enclave, backed by glorious, hand-painted Chinese silk screens.

The aunts were all seated, Tío Emilio standing, politely waiting for Cathy to settle. Dona Luisa patted the vacant seat at her side and Cathy sat quickly, her breath lodging beneath her breastbone in a ball of fire as Javier, declining a seat, stationed himself behind her, his long-fingered hands resting lightly on her shoulders.

How was she going to endure it? she asked herself frantically. She could cope more easily when he was in an evil mood. This softly seductive charm of his defeated her. And she couldn't tell him to go away, take his hands off her, not in front of Dona Luisa, who had gone to so much trouble to make this evening a success, and certainly not in front of the busy brightness of all those auntly eyes!

Taut as a guitar string, she longed for the evening to be over, to fly back to her room and hang over Juan's crib. Watching him, in his sleeping innocence, would bring her back to sanity. And then, with no ceremony at all, a slender young man appeared on the platform, his only accoutrements a guitar and a stool.

He put one booted foot on the stool and drew a few slow notes from the guitar, and the room was filled with the silence of expectation. Cathy held her breath, and felt the slightly increased pressure of Javier's fingers on the slender span of her collarbones.

And La Gitana appeared in silent explosion of colour, her traditional flamenco dress in a blaze of scarlet and black, scarlet carnations tucked into the glossy black hair drawn back from her strong-boned, white-skinned face.

Her head thrown back, she raised her right arm in a curve in front of her and circled the platform with short, rapid steps, her spine arched. The guitar sang.

And Cathy was lost, spellbound in the untamed sensuality of La Gitana's movements, in the passionate interplay between the guitar and castanets, the rhythmic stamp of her heels, her stylised, perfect interpretation of the dance, the flamenco music so vivid and haunting, sometimes harsh and sometimes mournful, but always subtle.

She tried to swallow the lump in her throat as the performance drew to an end and the gentle pressure of Javier's hands on her shoulders increased a little as his dark head bent, his lips close to her ear as he whispered, his voice thick, '*Así se baila*—that is how it should be danced.'

For a short moment Cathy allowed herself the luxury of leaning back, her half-averted head lifted so that her heated forehead touched the cool, sensual line of his mouth. He, too, had been affected by the performance, even though, as a Jerezano, he would certainly be no stranger to the flamenco.

But it had been her first time and the spell lingered, wrapping her in enchantment, allowing her to reach out and touch the soul of this fecund, savage, passionate land, allowing her to blindly, instinctively obey the commands of his hands as he eased her to her feet and guided her over the smooth cool marble and through one of the tall open windows.

Away from the now deserted *sala grande*, the soft night air enfolded them, the sultry warmth tempered by the first trailing patterns of mist, the cooling dew so vital to the grapes. And over the paved veranda he led her, down the shallow flight of steps, fitting his pace to

hers so that thigh clung to thigh in a slow, sensual
pavane, her body tucked into his as his strong right
arm encircled her tiny waist, his hand splayed possessively on the warm, feminine roundness of her hips.

'You enjoyed?'

In the dark silence his voice was low, more accented
than usual, thicker, and, still drifting in a dream, Cathy
answered honestly, 'I felt privileged.'

'Ah.' He led her on to a grassy path she had never
explored in daylight, flanked by ghostly, sweet-scented
oleanders, by stands of silvery eucalyptus. 'So you felt
the infection of passion? It is often so, with the very
best. They touch our souls.'

Their footsteps slowed, and they stopped, as if they
had been programmed to know each other's thoughts.
And he reached for her in the soft, secret darkness,
one hand stroking the pale gleam of her hair, the other
just lightly touching her throat, lifting her face to the
shadowed enigma of his.

How could Elena not have loved him? she thought,
her mouth trembling. How could she have wanted him
for mere material things only? She, with all her apparent beauty, youth and charm, could so easily have
translated his self-confessed lust into love. And to be
loved by such a man as he. . .

Tears shone in her drowning purple eyes, mirror
images of the glittering stars in the soft night sky, and
Javier's fingers stroked through her silky hair, cupping
her head, his sensual mouth closing one pale eyelid and
then the other, then drifting as lightly as a summer
breeze over her face, lingering for a tantalising moment
at the corner of her mouth then moving to the other,
to the soft indentation of her short upper lip. And then
withdrew, his mouth hovering a mere breath above her
own parted lips.

Her breath came in rapid, uneven gasps, her hands

finding their own way beneath the smooth fabric of his dinner-jacket, splaying against the cool, fine linen that covered his superb male body.

Tonight, so vital and yet so controlled, his impeccable masculine beauty had wrung her heart; his charm, his lover-like attention, had bewitched her. And the flamenco had added the final passionate stroke of magic that had her unable to think of anything but this moment, this fragment of time with the man she loved.

'Cathy, *mía*!' His voice had rough edges. Beneath the palms of her hands she felt his body shake, knew a moment of wild exultation as his arms went round her, dragging her into the warmth of his lithe body.

And she went with a whimper of pleasure, a whisper of sound that died as his mouth took hers and plundered, ravaging her senses, drawing forth a response she had not known she had to give as her hands straddled the beautiful shape of his head, her fingers lovingly tangled in the soft glossy darkness of his hair.

She was abandoned, wanton, and not ashamed as she had been before. How could she be? Love knew no shame, no holding back. Regrets might come later, but for now there was nothing beneath the Andalusian stars, the beneficent gauzy mist, but this one man and the magic of the moment.

Tonight, for a timeless moment that would live forever in her memory, and perhaps in some distant corner of his, he was hers, she thought exultantly as his breath sobbed against the tender warm hollow of her shoulder, his hands pushing the silky fabric aside, exposing the moon-gleam of her skin, her taut breasts proudly inviting the caress of his mouth.

'*Cariño. . .*' he groaned raggedly, his head dipping in wordless acceptance as his mouth found and devoured the pouting, inviting globes, making her back arch in wild ecstasy, her head falling back on her neck like a broken flower. He muttered in his own language, his words slurred, hot with passion, with a need that matched her own, a need that would kill if it weren't assuaged. And he gathered her into his arms, his long stride carrying her through the darkness.

And she clung to him, loving him, uncaring of where he was taking her, her mouth finding his jawline, nibbling, tasting the spice of the inevitable beard growth, her teeth nipping and teasing until his head dropped, his mouth finding hers and taking it, savagely marking her with his brand of possession.

And a few more purposeful yards and she was blinking owlishly at a summer-house twined with roses, dark blossoms everywhere, spilling their exotic perfume into the night. As silently as a great cat, he carried her over the threshold and set her gently on her feet, sliding her body down the length of his, and his voice was tight with a toughness he couldn't disguise as he stated, 'You know what will happen when I close this door behind us. If you want to leave, then say so now. I cannot promise to control myself if you allow things to go further and then back away.'

There was just enough starlight to reveal the hard planes of his face, the cruel slash of his mouth, and she remembered Elena and what she had done to him. But Elena had never loved him, only the things he could give her. Elena had been an indulged child. She, Cathy, loved him. And she was a woman, capable, she now knew, of passion, of the ability to give and go on giving. And she said quietly, but firmly enough for there to be no mistake, 'Close the door, Javier.' A hand lifted to touch his face and she felt the softening, the release of tension, and saw the wicked glint of his eyes as he gently swung the door into place and guided her through the voluptuous darkness to a softly padded lounger and laid her down, his deft hands removing the outward sophistication of silk, shaping her body with a touch that held reverence and desire in equal measure, his voice telling her things in a language she could not understand but would treasure for the rest of her life.

CHAPTER NINE

CATHY woke from two short hours of dream-haunted sleep as Juan bellowed for his first feed of the day. Crawling from her rumpled bed, she pulled a robe on over her nakedness and shuffled through to the nursery.

Images of the way she and Javier had been the night before, the way they had reluctantly left the summer-house at the break of day, were plastered indelibly on the inside of her skull and she had to blink to focus on the baby.

His chubby face was round with smiles, bellows forgotten as he saw her. He held out his little arms and she scooped him out of the crib, holding him possessively to her breast, dropping tiny, loving kisses on the top of his downy head.

How long had Rosa sat with him until she'd crept off to her own bed? The baby alarm had been switched through to the other girl's room, she'd noted when she'd returned. So what if he'd woken in the night — at two, or three or even four — and Rosa had been alerted, hurrying along the passages to attend to him, noticing, of course, her own absence?

Shame and guilt gnawed at the edges of her mind, but she was able to push them away as she propped Juan back in his crib and boiled water to mix his bottle, chattering to him all the time, refusing to let herself think beyond her small tasks.

But when the baby was contentedly feeding, securely held in her arms, she couldn't stop the relentless tide of self-recrimination.

Last night she had been bewitched, becoming an unthinking pagan in Javier's arms, not sparing a thought for what the others might have construed from their absence from what was left of the party Dona Luisa had given in her honour.

And Javier? Had his lovemaking been a final attempt to prove her a wanton—anyone's—unfit to bring up his nephew?

She couldn't think that of him, she couldn't! Or wouldn't, a nasty cold voice in her brain prompted. Was she refusing to admit the possibility because she wasn't strong enough to face the truth: that the way he had been—in turns tender, volcanically passionate, a sensualist delighting in giving and receiving pleasure, caring and gentle, teasing and intense—was nothing but a calculated ploy?

She was getting deeper and deeper into a mire of her own making, and digging herself out wasn't going to be easy. Perhaps not even possible.

She had lied to him, and he would never forgive that. She had fallen in love with him, and for that she would never forgive herself. And she was too muddled to attempt to think things through and was uselessly wishing herself and the baby a million light-years away when he walked through the door and she was reduced to feeling like a lovesick schoolgirl, afraid to meet his eyes for more than a tiny, embarrassed second.

If she could only know what was going on inside his head, what he thought of her. A trollop? She surely had lived up to Cordy's reputation with a vengeance, hadn't she just?

'I need to talk to you.' He sounded as weary as he looked, but he had a smile for Juan as he lifted him out of her arms and held him high above his head, his smile deepening as the baby crowed delightedly. 'Unfortunately, I've been called away on business. It might take a week, ten days — who knows?'

Cathy got out of the nursing chair stiffly, putting the empty bottle near the steriliser to be dealt with later. She should be jumping for joy because he would be gone for a time, giving her a breathing space, the opportunity to sort things out in her head and decide what to do. Confess everything and walk away, leaving the baby here? He would never lack for anything, either emotional or material. Yet could she make that sacrifice?

And should she be saying something about last night? Try to dismiss it lightly as just something that happened from time to time when the mood and the man were right? Show him she wasn't about to try to make capital out of it?

'You don't seem unduly distressed.'

The snap in his voice forced her to look at him, and her heart turned over. His face was austerely carved this morning and he looked remote, impeccable in a tailored pale grey suit and dark blue tie. And because she utterly, and perhaps foolishly, refused to allow anything to spoil her memories of last night, she proffered the ghost of a smile and said, 'Would it make any difference if I did? If business calls, then of course you must go. I have no claims on your time.'

The handsome features softened. Cathy had no way of knowing whether that was because of her tempered response or a reaction to the way Juan was crooning at him, testing the fit of the collar of his crisp white shirt with his tiny fingers, until he said softly, 'When we are married you will have every claim on my time. You and Juan will come before everything.'

He bent to prop the baby back in his crib, tucking a teething ring into his starfish hand, giving Cathy time to get her breath back. Come before everything? How could that be? And she found her regained breath knocked clear from her lungs again as he turned back to her, his hands gentle on her shoulders, forcing her to face him.

'This time I'm asking you to be my wife in the fullest sense of the word. After we last spoke on the subject I did a lot of thinking.' He lifted a hand to push her rumpled hair back from her brow, meeting her wide violet eyes with a wicked grey glint. 'I opened my heart to you, explained why I would never trust myself to love again. It is not something I reveal to everyone. Only you. However——' again the intensely revealing glint of devilish humour '—I quite see that it would hardly be fair—or safe—to ask you to live the life of a nun. And, to be honest, the idea of having children of my own begins to appeal—since you mentioned the possibility that you might want them. And last night proves that we are compatible. And do not blush so. . .'

Words were impossible as he kissed her slowly and softly, and Cathy was too stunned to do or say a single thing and could only stare at him, wide-eyed and boneless as he released her, straightening his tie.

'I expect a definite and positive answer when I return. Or may I have it now?'

His head tilted quizzically and she dropped her eyes beneath his steady, half-humorous regard, unable to answer, unble to think because of the tumultuous, raging desire to fling herself at him and accept him wholeheartedly. But such an unthinking acceptance would have far-reaching consequences, and she surely had to be grateful that his revised proposal had left her bereft of words when he gave her a resigned dip of his head and walked slowly to the door.

'I thought not. Your stubbornness both amuses and infuriates me. But in ten days, at most, I shall have my

answer. And I shall refuse to listen to anything but an
unreserved yes!' His parting smile was wicked, totally
unrepentant, full of a dazzling confidence that made
her shake to her soul.

He was so sure of her, of her willingness to agree —
especially after her wild and passionate responses to
his lovemaking — that he could see no obstacle to what
he wanted: Juan as a full member of his family, safe
within his benevolent control, with her willing body in
his bed as a bonus that couldn't be sniffed at!

He didn't know, couldn't know, that when she told
him the truth he wouldn't want her near him. He would
never forgive her for having lied to him, for forcing
him to propose that initial sterile marriage. His cruel
Spanish pride would not allow it.

A woman had made a fool of him before. He would
look on her lies as an attempt to do the same, and his
anger and disgust would be terrible. He would, she
knew, forgive most things. But never that.

'Why don't you go out and amuse yourself today?'
Rosa demanded as she walked into the sunny nursery.
And, meeting Cathy's blank look, persisted, 'For a
week you haven't set a foot outside except to take Juan
for his airing. You haven't made a single sketch, and
you are so very clever at it.'

'Don't nag, Rosa,' Cathy objected listlessly. It was
true that for the past seven days she had kept to her
room and the nursery, only emerging to take her meals
and push Juan around the gardens in his buggy, taking
care to steer well clear of the summer-house. But Rosa
couldn't begin to understand the pressure she'd been
under, the need to reach a firm decision regarding
Javier's new offer of marriage. Because, thankfully, he
hadn't repeated his premature announcement of their
wedding to anyone other than his mother.

And her self-inflicted isolation had been helped along when Dona Luisa had caught a head cold, refusing to come near her or the nursery until she was sure she was past the infectious stage.

'Someone has to nag,' Rosa retorted as Cathy laid Juan back in his crib for his morning nap. 'Maybe you are pining for Don Javier, but he won't be pleased to find you looking so dreary when he returns!'

That statement and the hint of mischief in the other girl's voice did it. Rosa was bright and intelligent, quite capable of drawing her own conclusions from the fact that she, the supposed mother of Francisco's child, had been brought to Spain and looked like being kept here for the duration, the fact that she and Javier had gone missing on the night of the reception, that she, Cathy, hadn't returned to her room until four the following morning.

Oh, Rosa, if only you knew! she thought wretchedly and knew her face had gone pink as she mumbled, 'I might go somewhere. Dona Luisa is over her cold. I saw her at breakfast and she told me she intends spending the entire afternoon with Juan.'

Rosa was quietly tidying the nursery, but when Cathy wandered through to her bedroom she left what she was doing and followed.

'Don Javier is expected back in the next couple of days, so why don't you get your hair done? There's a great salon on——'

'I'd rather go sketching,' Cathy interrupted quickly and falsely. She wouldn't; all her enthusiasm had disappeared in the anguish of knowing that crunch-time was growing nearer with every breath she took. But she wouldn't add fuel to Rosa's romantic conjectures by being seen to fall in with the suggestion that she pretty herself up while she waited for Javier's return.

'I'll take a trip to Cádiz,' she announced a shade wildly. From what she had read, it was a truly exotic place, and far enough away from Jerez. If, by sheer bad luck, Javier did return today, then she wouldn't be on hand for the show-down he'd promised. She'd do anything to defer that dreaded moment. 'I take it I can get a train from here? And you won't mind looking after Juan for me?'

'Of course I won't, you know that.' Rosa grinned. 'And why don't you go by sea? It's easy,' she tacked on, meeting the doubt in Cathy's eyes. 'I'll ring for a taxi to take you to Puerto de Santa María and you can take the *vapor* to Cádiz from there, and it's simple enough to get back by train to Jerez if the return boat sailings don't suit.'

So, an hour later, Cathy, armed with the canvas shoulder-bag containing her camera, notebook and sketching materials, wearing one of the cool outfits Dona Luisa had insisted on picking out for her, lifted her face to the breeze from the Atlantic as the sturdy boat chugged down the Rio Guadalete towards the open waters of the Bay of Cádiz.

For a few hours she was going to forget her troubles, she promised herself. If she didn't she would be a nervous wreck by the time Javier reappeared. A whole week of trying to reach a decision and stick to it had left her precisely where she'd been at the beginning— muddled, confused, loving him, knowing she wanted to be his wife more than anything in the world, knowing that before that could happen she would have to confess her sins. Knowing that when he learned the truth—that Juan's real mother had abandoned him in favour of her high-profile career—he would wash his hands of her, a mere aunt, and, moreover, tarred with the same brush as her infamous sister, and set about what he'd intended doing right from the first — legally adopting his dead brother's son.

Determinedly, she pushed all thoughts of Javier out of her head and glanced around her. The open upper deck of the boat was packed, almost every seat on the wooden benches occupied with chattering women, old men deep in impassioned dialogue and a smattering of German tourists with bulging back-packs.

Everyone had someone to talk to, but she thrust the beginnings of self-pity away, gave the Spaniard who came to collect her pesetas for the ride a huge smile, and made herself take an interest in her surroundings.

They were now chugging past the black hulls of three-masted fishing boats, rather like Arab dhows, moored near the mouth of the estuary, past ancient salt-stained rusty craft and forgotten half-sunken wrecks, side by side with smart pleasure boats. And further out into the bay, with the beaches and tall white apartment blocks disappearing into the haze behind them, Cathy caught her first sight of the white city of Cádiz and fished her camera out of her bag, then caught her breath at the sight of a huge cargo vessel looming out of the mist against the backdrop of the commercial dock.

Picking out the gleaming cruise liners, three busy tugs pulling a merchantman clear of the harbour and small fishing boats wallowing in the ensuing wash, all against a fascinating backdrop of tall cranes, modern office blocks and palm trees, kept her mind occupied. And it wasn't until they had disembarked and she had taken her life in her hands as she crossed the busy thoroughfare beyond the dock area and had gratefully subsided at a table outside an attractive bar and given her order for, '*Uno café solo, por favor,*' that all her miseries came rushing back.

The last time she had sat at such a table, outside a

bar, had been in Jerez. With Javier. And he had been angry because she had refused to accept his marriage proposal. Marriage in name only, at that stage of the game. Easy enough to refuse, out of hand. But his latest offer. . .

Crossly she dragged her mind away from him, drank her coffee, and set off haphazardly into the town, struck by the quality of the light, the brilliant whiteness, sometimes finding herself ambling along the stone sea walls, the waters of the bay glittering into the hazy distance, sometimes finding herself in a maze of narrow streets where the projecting balconies and latticed verandas almost met overhead. It was, she knew, reputed to be the oldest city in Europe and, to Cathy, the atmosphere still clung, a reminder of the wealthy merchants, the scholars, courtesans, the travelling kings with their vast retinues who had once made it the most sumptuous and cosmopolitan city on the coast.

She was hot and tired and hungry as she tried to find her way back to the docks. She hadn't put pencil to paper; she'd been too intent on scurrying around, gawping at this and that, trying to keep her mind involved with something other than the Jerezano.

And now the heat was killing her, her feet were killing her, and the colourful, filmy cotton skirt and loose-fitting, sleeveless black cotton blouse were sticking to her overheated body, and her long blonde hair was being tossed every which way by the sea breezes.

She scowled, dragging the irritating mass of hair away from her face, and Javier walked out of the Banco de Andalucia, paused on the hot pavement, and saw her.

And for her the world stood still when she saw the sudden brilliance of his smile, a kaleidoscope of impressions compounding the shock of seeing him here at all.

He was wearing a Continental-style light grey suit, the immaculate fit accentuating the narrowness of his hips, the rangy width of his shoulders and the length of his legs. Apart from being a superb example of the male of the species, he was special, so very special, and so much loved. And her smile trembled into radiance as he covered the short distance that separated them, a spurt of excitement twisting in her stomach.

'What are you doing here?' They both spoke at once, and Javier's warm grey eyes crinkled at the corners as he dipped his head.

'After you.'

'Oh—sketching,' she told him breathlessly, wondering why the moment she'd been dreading for a week had turned out to be so utterly magical. She only realised now just how desperately she'd missed him. He took her hand.

'I look forward to seeing them.'

'Well. . .' Impossible to explain that she hadn't done the merest squiggle. He might ask why. 'And you?' she changed the subject rapidly, her fingers clinging on to his as if her life depended on the contact.

'I had a little business here, which I decided to get over and done with on my way back to Jerez—and you,' he told her, his clever eyes searching her face. 'You look tired. Have you eaten?'

She shook her head. She was swamped by his overwhelming Spanish charisma, hopelessly out of her depth, trying to cope and failing dismally, because how could she walk away without fighting to take what he'd offered her? Surely if she could get him to listen to her explanations he would understand why she had lied to him. And forgive?

'Lunch, then,' he said and handed her into his parked Mercedes, joining the flow of traffic, and in no time at all, it seemed, they were seated at a table on a *terraza*,

overlooking San Roque and the blue Atlantic, surrounded by urns overflowing with flowers and shaded
by an awning of vines.

'*Ensalada ilustrada* followed by *langostinos a la plan-
cha*, of course,' Javier decided, disdaining the elaborate
menu, his eyes never leaving her face. His voice
purred. 'It would be a crime not to sample the produce
of the ocean when we are sitting almost on top of it.'

A prosaic enough remark, but the unbelievably sexy
tone of his voice, together with the unrelenting caress
of his fine eyes, would make a shopping list sound like
an erotic love poem.

Cathy melted inside, loving him, wanting him, took
a slow sip of her chilly *manzanilla* and decided to spoil
herself, enjoy an hour of unlooked-for bliss and worry
over what answer she would give him when he asked if
she was ready to agree to marry him when it actually
happened.

'You are beginning to relax. That is good,' he
approved lazily over the crisp mixed salad. 'It is my
company, or the wine, I wonder?'

His eyes, the curl of his mouth, told her that he
refused to believe any responsibility at all could be laid
before the wine, so, her eyes sparkling at him over the
rim of her glass, she told him, 'I always knew I could
get addicted to *manzanilla*.' And she held the cool
surface to her lips, pouting just a little, teasing.

And he growled, 'Little cat! When we are in a less
public place I will teach you differently.'

Her heart lurched over, fire beating through her
veins. With just a few words, the quality of expression
in those Spanish eyes, he could make her want to crawl
over the tabletop and curl up on his elegant lap, wrap
her arms around his neck and drag that sensual mouth
down to hers. . .

She knew that somehow she had unleashed a tiger,

but could she control it? Did she even want to try? Flirting with him like this was like playing with fire. One could die of third-degree burns, but hell, it would be worth it! And she watched in a haze of loving him as his long fingers dealt expertly with one of the giant king prawns, her lips parting softly as he held it to her mouth, sharp white teeth biting it in half.

And then, public place or not, he leant over the table, put the rest of the delicacy in his own mouth, and covered her lips with his.

An explosion of ecstasy, of fiery need, had her clutching his hands as they lay on the snowy tablecloth, and his fingers curled possessively around hers as he asked against her trembling mouth, 'You will marry me?'

'Yes,' she breathed, and didn't regret it. Her entire system was burning up with wanting him, loving him; her thought processes gone up in smoke, disenabling her brain. No room for regrets, misgivings, any kind of coherent thought. No room for anything in her head but the blazing brand of her love for him.

'Good. That is good.' Again the light, earth-shattering pressure of his lips against hers and then he withdrew, leaning back, his eyes dancing as he told her, 'I could have killed someone when that call came through, dragging me away. After the night we had spent together I was sure I could persuade you to my way of thinking. Unfortunately——' his wide shoulders rose in a slight, fatalistic shrug '—the best I could do was revise my proposal and give you time to think it over. Time to bolster up all that stubbornness of yours.' He smiled at her suddenly, like a great big pussy-cat. 'I spent the last seven days anguishing for nothing!'

Had he anguished, just as she had? No, impossible. Quite impossible. She had just agreed to be his wife and, naturally, he felt a few compliments were due. If she had adamantly refused to do as he wanted he would merely have given that throw-away shrug of his, written the whole idea off, and gone back to his original plan, translating all those threats into action. He had all the Campuzano wealth behind him, and money meant power. Lots of it.

But she wasn't going to let that dark cloud shadow this one shining hour. All she wanted was to savour this moment, savour him, the food, the wine, the perfumed flowers, the murmur of the glittering sea, the warmth of the air as it filtered through the vines. She wanted to bask in his undivided attention, in his considerable ability to charm, to clutch on to her love for him as a child might hold the perfect symmetry of a single snowflake in the palm of its hand, knowing that it would melt away, its loveliness transmuted into a patch of grubby water.

And he charmed her, filling her mind and body with wonder, the glorious, special wonder of him. When coffee appeared he excused himself. 'I won't be a moment, *enamorada*. Then I am taking you home.'

And, watching him walk away between the other tables, Cathy felt her body go stiff with shock, her eyes widening unseeingly as she thought, What have I done? Oh, God, what have I done?

All week long she had agonised over what she should do and had finally reached a decision she had felt she should stick to—no matter if the consequences had been bitter. She should have told him everything, explained exactly why she had lied, and then, and only then, asked if he still wanted to marry her.

That he wouldn't had been a risk she had steeled herself to take, knowing that if—by some crazy miracle—he did they would have a wonderful future together. He didn't love her, she knew that. He believed himself incapable of ever loving anyone. But he wanted her physically, and he wanted to adopt Francisco's child, and, out of that, he could have learned to love her a little, surely?

He was wearing a very self-satisfied look when he returned to the table, and Cathy gulped down the dregs of her coffee, hiding behind the cup. She was going to have to tell him the truth on the journey back to Jerez. It was the last opportunity she would get, and she wasn't looking forward to it. But it would be unthinkable to allow him to make wedding announcements to all and sundry. If she delayed the truth until later he would feel he had been trapped. And rightly so.

Even so, it was difficult to find the courage to begin, find a suitable opening in his light-hearted conversation as they made the return journey by road.

'You're very quiet, *querida*.' The brief glance held a query and she looked away from him quickly, her eyes fastened on the verges as they came to a halt at a busy intersection.

'It's the heat,' she excused. 'Not to mention the sherry.' The car was air-conditioned and she'd had only one small glass of the wine. His company had been intoxicating enough. She turned the subject quickly, babbling, 'I just love all your wild flowers.' She could identify tiny purple irises, periwinkles, horsetails of wild barley and blossoms that looked like purple bells and others that looked like tiny white stars and she went on with a rush, her voice too high and thin, 'You don't find so many wild flowers in England. Everything gets sprayed with herbicide; the farmers——'

'You are nervous,' he cut in as the car shot forward. 'There is no need to be. As my wife you will be accepted by everyone, respected and loved.' He sounded at his most lordly, as if anyone who had the temerity to question his choice of wife would live to regret it, and she blinked back a scalding tear. She loved him so much, even at his most impossible. And she was going to have to confess now. Right now. Then she sagged in relief as he gave her a breathing space.

'When I left you at the restaurant it was to phone home and let Madre know I had met up with you and would be taking you to the *finca* for a couple of days. We need just a little time on our own before we're flung into the happy chaos of wedding arrangements, when we will hardly have time to snatch a word together, never mind anything else.'

She turned her head, meeting the warmth of his eyes before he returned them to the road, and knew he had registered the way her face had gone pink at his mention of that 'anything else'.

The tension that had been gripping her so tightly was suddenly, gloriously, released. At the *finca*, just the two of them, she would have all the time she needed to put her case. To try and make him understand, forgive her. He would forgive her, wouldn't he? She didn't know how she would cope with the rest of her life if he didn't, not with the threat of losing Juan hanging over her as well.

And later, sitting at the oval table in the lofty farmhouse dining-room, over the remains of an excellent dinner, Cathy gave thanks to the kindly fates that had led the Jerezano to decide they needed time alone together. He'd been amazingly gentle and thoughtful with her, installing her in the room she'd used before, telling her to rest, take a shower, take her time, because they had the whole of the evening before them, the whole of the next two days.

And devilish, too, as he'd come back moments later with a silky robe tucked over his arm.

'Mine. You don't have a change of clothing here. Put the things you're wearing out for Paquita to launder and use this.' She caught the robe he tossed lightly to her. A slither, a whisper, a rustle of fine silk. And she went hot all over as he retreated, his eyes wicked with his parting shot, 'And I don't intend you to be using that for long, either, *querida*. I've given Paquita instructions to bring dinner forward and make herself scarce. After that, the night will be ours.'

And now Cathy's pulses were jumping out of control, because the look in his eyes told her he wanted her, and she had to tell him, and tell him now. And he gave her exactly the opening she wanted because, instead of coming to take her in his arms, as she had been so sure he would, he said quietly, 'There should be no secrets between a man and a woman when they make their wedding vows, *querida*. I have opened my past to you, told you the details of my ill-fated marriage to Elena. Do you have anything to say to me? There should be honesty, don't you think?' He was leaning back, lids heavy, thick lashes shading his eyes. He brooded quite beautifully, Cathy thought on a stab of anguished loving. And this was the ideal opportunity to put everything straight between them.

She looked down quickly, fiddling with the stem of her wine glass as she gathered her courage. Yes, he had been honest, told her the truth about his first marriage, been open about the fact that he believed he could never truly love a woman, had decided that love as an emotion was a mere wild fancy, a more socially acceptable word for lust. And, with one traumatically embittering experience behind him, he had deliberately set out to seduce her on the night of the reception, just to make sure that she wasn't another Elena — all promise and no substance.

So in her own defence she would have to tell him about Donald, even if it did give him an insight into the way she felt about him. Beginning with that, it would pave the way to the other, more tricky revelation.

She took in a deep breath and lifted her head to meet his brooding eyes, the slight, encouraging smile that lingered on his sensual lips.

'I once believed myself in love,' she said quietly, wondering how he was going to take this. From what she knew of his arrogant pride he could be the type of man who would expect his wife to be an innocent, refusing to take second-hand goods. But, as he had stated, there had to be honesty. 'We were students together, years ago, and I think he thought he loved me, too. We became lovers, and I thought I was frigid because the act meant so little.' Quick fumblings in the dark, almost painful, and leaving her feeling used and ashamed. Leaving him feeling the same, too, if the way he had uncomfortably avoided her eyes on the following morning had been anything to go by. 'It didn't take long before we both realised our relationship wasn't going to work. We stayed friends, though, until he went to work in the North after qualifying.'

Coming to terms with her mistake had taken a time. She had been wary of men, of making the same mistake twice, because she had always been too fastidious to enjoy casual sex. And her mother had died and she'd been busy trying to keep Cordy on the rails, and she had got into the habit of believing she had a low sex drive.

Her teeth bit into the soft fullness of her lower lip, wondering if he had made the connection. She had as good as told him that Donald had been her only lover until now, an opening into the truth of her real relationship to Juan. Believing her to be the mother of Francisco's child, being willing to take her on for the sake of that child, had been one thing. Knowing she had no more rights over Juan than he did, and still wanting to take on spoiled innocence, would be another. But all he said was, 'With me you discovered you were far from frigid. We were—explosive.' His eyes glinted, as if he were reliving the memory of that night, and she shuddered, remembering too, her mouth going dry as one black brow lilted gently upwards. 'But there is more. . .'

There was. Much more. And somehow, crazily, she knew it was going to be all right, that he would hear her out with patience and that his judgement would not be harsh. She took a calming breath and opened her mouth, and her words of explanation were pushed back into her throat as the bell on the door to the farmhouse jangled and Javier snarled, 'Cristo!' gave her a tight-lipped shrug, and strode out of the room, the look of barely leashed anger in the hard set of his shoulders boding no good for whoever had disturbed them at such an inopportune moment.

Cathy felt like swearing herself. She just knew in her bones that the moment had been as right as it ever could be. But Javier had insisted that Paquita and Tomás take the rest of the evening off, and they had retired early to their own quarters, so he would have to see to his unwelcome visitor himself.

She smiled wryly, getting to her feet and beginning to stack the used dishes. The visitor, whoever, would soon be sent packing; his eyes would be blinking for days over the swiftness of his dismissal.

But she was wrong. Quite how wrong she didn't realise until she glanced up and saw Cordy standing in the doorway, a tiny smile on her perfectly made-up features, her voice pure treacle as she cried, 'Darling— I came as soon as I got your letter. I dropped everything and came. You and my baby needed me, so here I am!'

CHAPTER TEN

'HE IS spectacular!' Cordy flopped down on the end of the bed and pushed her fingers through the artfully disarrayed rumple of her streaked blonde mane. 'Why didn't you write sooner?' she wanted to know, her head tilted as she gave Cathy a hard blue stare. 'I never dreamed something had happened to Francisco — you should have told me as soon as you knew.'

'I didn't think you'd be interested,' Cathy retorted grimly. 'You were so full of your new Hollywood career. What happened about that?' And she had wanted to keep her sister right out of it. At that time all she'd been concerned about had been seeing the adoption through, with Cordy's full blessing and consent. She hadn't wanted Javier to know the truth.

Cordy waved a dismissive hand. The glamour of a film career obviously took second place to the fruits of muscling in on the Campuzano family — which was what she'd set her sights on ever since she'd learned of her pregnancy — Cathy decided bitterly, shooting her sister an exasperated glance. Why had she had to turn up at that delicate moment?

Another hour and she would have told Javier the truth and everything would have been resolved between them one way or another. And because Cordy had decided not to wait at the house in Jerez, discovering their whereabouts from a no doubt highly confused Dona Luisa, Javier despised her. She had seen it in his eyes.

'Anyway, all's well that ends well, as the saying goes.' Cordy smiled serenely, unbuttoning the short-sleeved, precisely fitted acid-yellow jacket she wore over her tight white skirt and tossing it heedlessly to the floor, her body displayed to seductive advantage in a low-necked, gossamer-fine sleeveless top. 'I dropped everything as soon as I read your letter and learned he was willing to marry his nephew's mother for his dead brother's sake. Though why you said you were Johnny's mother I'll never understand. Unless——' her eyes narrowed '—you hoped to carry it off until after the wedding and then take a big fat divorce settlement.' She stood up, smoothing down her skirt. 'And he would have divorced you when he inevitably found out you'd lied. He was livid when I told him who I was.'

Cathy didn't have to be reminded. Her stomach twisted sickeningly. He would have only had to take one look at the vision of glamour on his doorstep to know that she was the model, Cordelia Soames, he'd seen tangled up with his brother on that long-ago night in Seville. And his features had been frozen into a mask of contempt as he'd followed Cordy into the dining-room and tersely instructed, 'Cathy, rouse Paquita and ask her to make a room ready for your sister,' insisting, 'Now, if you please,' as she'd opened her mouth to tell him she could explain everything, her violet eyes pleading.

Her backbone stiff with pride, she had swept out of the room. She wouldn't try to plead with him a second time. The look on his face had flayed her, and she wouldn't let anyone see how hurt and shocked she was. And she would make up Cordy's damn bed herself. No need to drag Paquita away from her television set and hurl her head-first into this hornets' nest.

And now Cordy was slipping her feet back into her high-heeled acid-yellow shoes, checking the seams of her stockings were straight, and Cathy, as ever, felt a frump beside her elegant, beautiful sister, especially when she swept her cold blue eyes over the robe Javier had lent her.

'All ready for bed, I see. Well, you pop along while I go and find the magnificent Campuzano you've been hiding away. I'll ask him to bring me up to date on how my darling baby's been progressing during my unavoidable absence—someone had to earn enough to keep the three of us, and you couldn't.'

So that was the way she was going to play it, Cathy thought, nearer to hating her sister than she had ever been. She would have liked to rip those elegant clothes from her back and remind her of the time when she hadn't been able to bring herself to do the smallest thing for the tiny, adorable creature she had brought into the world. Brought into the world, moreover, with one aim in mind—earning herself a place in the wealthy Campuzano family.

But Cathy knew she was in an over-emotional state and that if she set about Cordy, either physically or verbally, she would regret it deeply when her fraught emotions were back under control again. So she contented herself with warning, her voice dull with banked-down pain, 'He only offered to marry me because I wouldn't be bribed into allowing him to adopt the baby. He wants Johnny—or Juan, as he prefers to call him—brought up as his heir, as a Campuzano and a Spaniard. He'll try to bribe you, too.'

'Bribe me?' Cordy raised one finely plucked eyebrow. 'I don't think so. If it took him a few weeks to get to the point of proposing marriage to you—for the child's sake, of course—then I can bring him to the point in a few days, wouldn't you say?' She walked slowly to the full-length mirror and delicately moved her hands over her svelte body, watching herself, her smile brilliant as she met Cathy's tormented, reflected eyes. 'No, I don't think bribery will enter his handsome head, do you?'

For long moments after Cordy had left the room Cathy stood with her eyes closed, fighting back tears. She felt like a puppet, a lifeless lump of wood. And whoever was pulling her strings had no liking for her at all. In the space of a few moments she had lost everything.

The Jerezano viewed her with deep contempt. He would believe she had tried to make a fool of him, accepting his proposal of marriage under false pretences, laughing at him up her sleeve. If she had been able to make him understand exactly why she had lied—because she had been afraid, at first, that he would take the baby she had cared for and loved ever since his birth—then he might have forgiven her. But, in these circumstances, he never would, and she had lost the chance of teaching him to love her a little over the years to come, the chance of bearing his children. She had lost all hope of adopting the baby, too. Cordy would see to that, even if Javier didn't.

Little Juan was back to being a pawn. Cordy would grimly cling on to him, knowing he was her admittance ticket to the wealthy and élite Campuzano family. And the little darling deserved better than that!

And then the tears came, pouring unstoppably down her cheeks as she fumbled out of the room she'd made ready for Cordy and into her own. Even now her sister would be sweet-talking Javier, explaining how she, the broken-hearted mother, had bravely gone back to work to earn enough to keep her child, leaving him in the safe hands of her older sister, or so she had thought. Cordy could be very convincing, Cathy thought bleakly as she cried herself to sleep.

* * *

'Wake up and stop skulking. I've almost convinced Javier that you didn't lie out of malice, merely stupidity and frustrated maternal hang-ups.'

The bright and bouncy voice was too much to bear, and Cathy turned her face into her pillow. Her head was pounding and her eyes felt raw and swollen. She didn't want to get up. Ever.

She could just imagine what Cordy had said to Javier, how distaste would have darkened his eyes, how his inbred politeness would have stilled his razor-sharp tongue, how his Andalusian pride would have had him dismissing the subject of her treachery as if it were beneath his notice.

'And guess what. . .' Cathy felt the mattress dip as Cordy sat on the edge of the bed. 'I was up with the lark—in the circumstances I thought it best—and after a bit of poking around I found our sensational host schooling a horse. God, he looked magnificent! All mean and moody manhood! Scrummy! And, wouldn't you know it, his stud is approved by the Royal School of Equestrian Art, which means, apparently, that he can provide suitable, pure-bred Spanish horses—I think he called them *cartujanos*—for their selection. And I'm pretty sure I've talked him into taking me to see a performance—there's one today, as luck would have it—and lunch after, naturally. He had to pop into town—on business, he said—but he told me he wouldn't be long. That's why I've come to chew over the fat with you. I won't have time if he's taking me out later.'

'You have been busy!'

The snap in Cathy's voice was muffled by the pillow, and even with her eyes squeezed shut she could see her sister's throw-away shrug, the glint in her hard blue eyes as she countered, 'It pays to show an interest.'

Pays. It would always come down to that, wouldn't

it? As far back as she could remember Cordy had always been calculating; everything she did or said had an ulterior motive. Her own interests would always come first.

So now wasn't the time to give way to her own feelings of loss and despair. Cathy struggled up against the pillows and said, her voice tight, 'I would have thought you'd prefer to see Johnny, rather than the horses — no matter how brilliantly they perform. You haven't seen him for months.'

'First things first. I always get my priorities right; you know that, or should do by now. If Javier is prepared to marry the mother of Francisco's child, then I'm not going to sit back and let him hitch up to the wrong woman by mistake, am I? Besides, the kid's being well looked after, and you're not exactly hanging over his cot, are you? So don't be such a damned prig!'

It had been the first night ever she'd spent away from the baby, and there was no way she was going to let Cordy know just why she and Javier had been here, alone — that it had been his idea to take a couple of days to be together before the frantic merry-go-round of wedding arrangements took them over.

An idea she had willingly fallen in with, because it would have given her all the time she needed to put things straight, to give him the opportunity — if he had wanted it — to retract his proposal with no one, except Dona Luisa, who would have been discreet and understanding, being any the wiser.

'Did you and Javier discuss the child at all?' Cathy demanded, and gritted her teeth together at Cordy's purring reply.

'No, why should we? Your letter told me what he wanted: the kid, for the sake of his dead brother and family honour and all that stuff. We had other things to say to one another. I didn't try to ram it down his throat—apart from telling him how devoted I am to my baby, how I'd missed him, and how broken-hearted I was because I had to leave him with you while I earned our living in the only way I knew how.'

'I could slap you!' Cathy growled, and meant it. 'Don't pretend you've forgotten how you couldn't be bothered to do a single thing for your baby, how you told me to go ahead and adopt him because you didn't want him! And tell me something, did you deliberately try to get pregnant when you realised that Francisco came from a wealthy, respected, high-profile family? The type of family who had too much honour to sweep their bastards under the carpet?'

Cordy abandoned the satisfied examination of her beautiful white hands, her eyes narrowing as they roved over Cathy's flushed face, her voice cool as she jeered, 'My, you have changed, haven't you? There was a time when you would have fallen over backwards to give me the benefit of every doubt, when you couldn't see any bad in anyone. Remember Donald? Your first true love. You couldn't see any bad in him either, could you? It was pitiful.' She stood up, her eyes scornful. 'He was only after you for one thing, and when he'd got it he found it wasn't worth the trouble. He told me. He also told me he couldn't believe we were sisters, that I must have got your share of what it takes to please a man. And no, if you must know, I didn't get pregnant on purpose.' She walked over to the mirror above the dressing-table and began stroking Cathy's brush through her tumbling blonde hair. 'I'd forgotten my pills, left them behind when I went on that shoot. And if I hadn't got tipsy at that party it wouldn't have happened. But it did. My first thoughts were to get an abortion, my second were how I could make it work for me. The rest, as they say, you know.'

Only she hadn't known everything, Cathy thought

bitterly. Even then she had been full of admiration for
the way her sister had bravely put her career on ice,
choosing to have the baby and care for it herself, even
if the father hadn't wanted to know. Even then she'd
been blind, choosing to think the best and never the
worst. And, looking at Cordy now, the sleek white
trousers and sleeveless corn-coloured vest emphasising
her beautiful body, she could hardly believe that
anyone that lovely could possibly be so self-centred
and hard.

But she could be very convincing, Cathy reminded
herself. Had Javier fallen for the distorted, sweetened
version of herself? The knowledge that Donald, who,
she had believed, had always been her friend, even
after their short-lived love-affair had ended, had
spoken so hurtfully of her to her own sister paled into
total insignificance against the much greater hurt of
knowing that Javier had wiped her from his mind so
easily, turning, apparently, to Cordy.

He had never pretended to love her; he had told her
the truth when he'd said he didn't believe he was
capable of loving any woman. For him there could only
be desire and physical need; his heart could never be
given.

But had their perfect lovemaking meant so very
little? He had not even bothered himself to seek her
out, demand to know why she had lied, tried to get at
the truth. Now he knew she wasn't his nephew's mother
she had no place in his life. And Cordy would make a
far more ornamental wife. And, as she swung her long
legs out of bed, determined to leave as soon as possible,
Cordy confirmed her dreary thoughts, turning from
scrutinising her perfect reflection to announce, 'God,
you look awful!' Her head tilted assessingly. 'You've
been crying. Don't tell me you actually fell for our

gorgeous host. You didn't really think you could marry him and hope to get away with the deception, did you?'

'You've got to be joking!' Cathy denied doing anything quite that foolish. After all, she did have some pride. 'Would I have written to you in the first place, if that was what I had in mind?'

'Good.' For a moment Cordy's eyes softened. 'I would hate you to get hurt. You might not believe it, but it's true. I owe you, and don't think I don't know it. And, for what it's worth, after Javier and I are married you'll always be welcome. I do know how much the kid means to you. So don't get upset; you can see him as often as you like, and you'll be the best aunty a kid could have.'

In spite of everything, Cathy's eyes misted, because just for that moment they had been sisters again, sharing old bonds and affections. But then, inevitably, Cordy put everything back to normal as Cathy reached for the laundered clothes Paquita must have brought to her room early this morning while she was still asleep.

'And by the way, you could do with losing a stone, if not more. Work at it, why don't you?' she said and swept out of the door, wiggling the fingers on one hand, wearing her pussy-cat smile.

Showered and dressed in the freshly laundered clothes, Cathy felt better. Not much, but marginally. She knew what she had to do, and she had to be sensible about it.

She had always been the sensible one, her mother had often said. Level-headed, good in a crisis, good to lean on. Right now Cathy felt none of these thing and ached to have someone to lean on herself. But that wasn't possible, so she squared her shoulders and went to find Cordy.

She was sitting in the courtyard in the shade of a pomegranate tree, the scarlet blossoms dancing in the brilliant sunlight. She had changed already and looked coolly beautiful in a tailored white linen suit, and she asked, 'Do I look OK for a horsy affair? Should I wear something more sporty?'

'You look lovely, and you know it,' Cathy said bleakly, sitting down for just a moment to say her goodbyes. 'Did he definitely say he would take you?'

It hurt terribly. Once he had made a throw-away offer to take her to a performance of the world famous high dressage, to see, as he had said, 'How the Andalusian horses dance'. It was the one thing she had vowed not to miss during her time in Jerez. But nothing, it seemed, ever went to plan, and Cordy was saying, 'He certainly didn't veto the idea when I suggested it. And I know I impressed him with my enthusiasm over that horse he was schooling. He just said he had to go to town on business but would be back quite soon.'

Which made Cathy want to get up and run and hide. But she wouldn't let herself be such a coward. She had to see him one last time, to accept again all that contemptuous anger she had seen on his face last night.

She shifted restlessly on the seat, knowing he wouldn't want to set eyes on her again. If he had, even if only to roar his disgust for what she had done, he had had plenty of opportunity. Instead he had coldly ignored her existence, spending his time with Cordy, getting her off-kilter version of events, getting to know her, making plans for spending time with her today.

So no, he wouldn't want to see her, and he wouldn't want to listen to her apologies. But she needed to make them. She wouldn't be able to live with herself if she didn't tell him how genuinely sorry she was for having lied to him. More sorry than he could ever know.

She closed her eyes, the hot, spicy scent of geraniums

mingling with the sweeter, headier perfumes of roses and lilies, the subtler tones of the dusty white soil that nurtured the vines bringing a lump to her throat, evoking the soul of the land she had come to love in such a short time, almost as much as she loved the man who was the physical embodiment of Andalusia's pride and passion—the Jerezano.

For a brief few hours she had allowed herself to believe in the possibility of a future here, with Javier and Juan. She had believed a dream and it had turned into a nightmare, a dark fantasy of pride and honour, with an iron will on one side and her own foolish deceit on the other. Not a mixture that could ever make a cohesive whole, and suddenly she was anxious for Cordy.

Her eyes opened, winging to the cool composure of her sister's face, a composure belied by the impatiently tapping toe of one spindly-heeled black leather shoe. And she said quickly, 'Don't pin too many hopes on an offer of marriage coming from Javier. He doesn't have a high opinion of English women.' Elena had been English, and after the way she, Cathy, had behaved he must view the female half of the race with deep mistrust, not to mention contempt. 'And after I strung him along——' she felt herself redden as she shouldered the blame squarely '—he's probably off the whole idea of marrying for Juan's sake.'

'It's a possibility,' Cordy admitted. 'But then I always hedge my bets. What brought me here in such a hurry was the knowledge that the Campuzanos haven't washed their hands of Francisco's child and his mother—me. There's money there—lots of it—and I intend to see the kid get his share. Me too, of course. And I must admit that when I read that he'd offered to marry you, thinking you were me, I was intrigued. But the screen tests came out well and my agent's confident

I'm going to be offered a contract, so I wasn't actually thinking of marriage, as such, and kissing any hopes of an acting career goodbye. Not until I met him. I wouldn't mind putting the contract on hold for twelve months or so and being a dutiful mother and wife if he was warming my bed at night. You know, I thought Francisco was dishy, but he was nowhere near Javier's league.' She glanced at her watch, her face clouding. 'What's keeping him? We'll miss that performance if he doesn't turn up in the next ten minutes.'

'If he said he had a business appointment, then he could be gone for days,' Cathy told her from her own experience, and Cordy gave her a scornful look.

'That's right, cheer me up!' Then, her eyes narrowing against the harsh rays of the sun, 'What are you going to do? You can't stay here. Javier might be too polite to ask you to leave, but he can't want you here.'

'You think I don't know that? As soon as I've apologised for lying to him I'll go.'

'Oh, I don't think that's a very good idea — apologising, I mean. If he'd wanted an apology he would have confronted you by now. From his attitude last night and again this morning I'd say he'd ram the words back down your throat. Besides. . .' The wheedling note that Cathy remembered from years back took over Cordy's voice. It meant her sister wasn't as sure of herself as she pretended. 'It could make things awkward. Thanks to you, his opinion of the female sex must be pretty low by now. If you make his mood any blacker, where will that leave me?'

She had a point, Cathy conceded reluctantly. She knew she owed it to Javier, and to herself, to make that apology, even if he did ram the words back down her throat. But she didn't want to jeopardise the negotiations over Juan's future. Javier and Cordy had to reach some kind of understanding — whether marriage was included or not. She would be acting selfishly if she stayed around to see him for one last time. She had already done far too much damage.

'Perhaps you're right.' She got stiffly to her feet. She could always write later, when the dust had settled, and try to explain her motives. 'I'll go and find Tomás and ask if he'll drive me into town. I need to pack and say goodbye to Juan and Dona Luisa.'

'I can do that—pack your things. I could send them on. And why bother saying goodbye? I shouldn't think Javier's mother would relish the embarrassment. She looked pole-axed when I arrived there yesterday evening and explained who I was. She probably thinks you're mad!' She got to her feet, too. 'And saying goodbye to the kid would only upset you, and wouldn't mean a thing to him, not at his age. Besides, you can see him whenever you want; I told you that. So why not go straight to the airport? Have you got enough money?'

She hadn't, but she could use her credit card. She had stopped availing herself of that convenience when her income had become so irregular. But, just this once, she would have to do it.

It was on the tip of her tongue to ask what the hurry was, but she was saved the trouble when the big Mercedes swung through the wide arch in the courtyard wall and Javier got out, slamming the door behind him with unnecessary force, his grave features tight with simmering anger.

'Now look what you've done!' Cordy spat in her ear. 'Just seeing you hanging around has put him in a foul mood. Why couldn't you have done the decent thing and pushed off?'

But Cathy hardly heard her, her concentration entirely on the powerful, striding figure of the man she loved. She felt the ground tilt beneath her and had to call on all her mental and physical resources to keep upright. Her heart was beating like a drum, out of control, and the look on his dark features was enough to tell her that he would never listen to a word she said by way of an apology—or anything else, come to that.

'We've been saying goodbye,' Cordy explained with a sweet smile. 'Cathy's as good as on her way. She was just about to ask your man to drive her to the airport.'

'If you'll wait in the car, Cordelia, I won't keep you a moment. I have a few things to say to your sister.' His voice was harsh, the velvet patina rubbed away by his deep contempt, and although he spoke to Cordy his hard eyes never wavered from Cathy's anguished features. The exciting, charming, devilish man who had wrung that unthinking acceptance from her in Cádiz might never have existed.

From the corner of her eye she watched Cordy glide over to the car, her smile completely feline as she settled herself in the passenger seat. Cathy licked her lips. Her mouth had gone too dry. She couldn't get that overdue apology out if her life depended on it, she thought frantically and found herself quailing in miserable guilt beneath the bitter steel of his eyes as he threatened, 'So you were running away? Well, I tell you this—move one foot off the *finca* before I say you may, and I will sue you for breach of promise.' He snapped hard fingers in the air, his eyes still drilling into her soul, and Tomás appeared from somewhere on the run. Tersely Javier spoke in rapid Spanish, and Tomás nodded, flicking her a rueful glance before retreating. 'You will stay here until I return,' he stated, his eyes daring her to utter one single word. 'I have harsh things to say,' he promised savagely. 'And you will listen to each one of them.' He swung on his heels his shoulders rigid. 'And then, and only then, you may do as you please.'

* * *

Javier and Cordy had been gone for hours. Not even a very late, extravagantly long lunch could have kept them for this length of time, Cathy thought crossly as she stared at the dusty white road that led down from the *finca*. If he was trying to punish her, he was succeeding. Or perhaps, she thought on a wave of desolation, he was finding Cordy's company so entrancing that he had forgotten she existed!

No matter, she thought, suddenly mutinous; she would not wait a single moment longer. He couldn't order her around; she wouldn't stand for it. She was sick of feeling guilty and suitably chastened. And sue her for breach of promise? She'd like to see him try!

She would ask Tomás to drive her to Jerez, where she would take her leave of Dona Luisa, Rosa and Juan and then book into a cheap hotel for the night. No matter if it did upset her, as Cordy had prophesied; she just had to hold her baby in her arms for one last time.

The thought of never seeing the child again—because Javier would demand to adopt him, she knew he would, whether or not he wanted Cordy along too—was unbearable.

She sucked air deep into her lungs and strode off towards the farmhouse, trying not to cry, telling herself that she had long ago admitted that the Campuzanos could give the child a much brighter future than she could have done.

Collecting her handbag from her room, she ran Tomás to earth in the kitchen. But her simple request brought an embarrassed, '*Lo siento, señorita*. Don Javier, he say stay here.' And Paquita, turning from the sink where she was industriously washing vegetables, said a whole lot in Spanish which Cathy couldn't understand, but the tone of voice, in any language, was clearly a 'cheer up and don't worry' one, the same tone of voice she'd used when she'd served her with the lavish lunch she hadn't been able to eat.

With a murmured and dignified '*Gracias*', Cathy swept out. So the dark devil thought he had her trapped, cowering here until he chose to return to deliver the harsh words he had warned her were coming. If his threats to sue her wouldn't hold her here, then the lack of transport would. Because she had no doubt at all that he'd had Tomás relay his instructions to every other worker on the estate. Well, was he in for one huge surprise!

If she couldn't hitch a lift when she reached the main road, she would walk. Even if it took her all night! Tucking her handbag securely under her arm, she headed away from the house, knowing her emotions were definitely unbalanced but not caring, because only by hating him, showing him he couldn't make her stay where she didn't want to be, could she prevent herself from dissolving into a guilt-ridden mess of misery.

And even though she tried hard not to, she couldn't help wondering what Javier and Cordy were doing, why they had spent so many hours away. Making plans for Juan's future, that was for sure. Javier would have no trouble convincing Cordy that it would make sense for him to adopt the child and bring him up as his heir. And if Cordy gave any sign of objecting would he add the inducement of marriage?

Why not? Since he believed himself incapable of truly loving a woman, following his dreadful experience with Elena, he had been willing to marry the model's much less beautiful sister — the one who didn't know how to please a man! Had she pleased him on that magical night when he'd transformed the world into paradise for her?

What if he'd been disappointed? What if he was,

even now, saying the sort of things about her that Donald had confided to Cordy?

It didn't bear thinking about and, anyway, it couldn't matter less. Not now.

Cathy stumbled on the dusty track, startling a little owl on a nearby fence post. It flew away into the dusk, its harsh call emphasising the loneliness of the empty landscape. She was beginning to question the wisdom of trying to hitch a lift into Jerez. Soon it would be completely dark, and she hadn't even reached the road. But any decision to admit defeat and return to the farmhouse was taken out of her hands when the snarl of an engine and the glare of headlights had her leaping for the side of the track.

'*Por Dios!*' That and a string of violent-sounding Spanish expletives had her wanting to clap her hands over her ears. But she did no such thing. She stood her ground, even though her knees were shaking, as Javier leapt out of the Mercedes and planted himself in front of her, his feet hardly seeming to touch the ground. And tension kept his lean body taut, his lips drawn back against his teeth as he snarled, 'Where the hell do you think you're going?'

Anger and pain ripped through her. He looked as if he wanted to kill her. The change from the man who had seduced, bewitched and fascinated her, the man who had stolen her heart, making it his own for all time, was shattering. And all for the sake of a protective lie. He didn't know the meaning of tolerance, compassion or understanding; all he cared about was his damned Spanish pride. And she shouted right back to him, not caring if Cordy was sitting in the car, lapping up the scene with that pussy-cat smile on her face.

'To Jerez, to pack my things. Where else?'

'How?' he barked straight back. 'Where is your broomstick, witch?'

'Since you told all your people not to take me anywhere, I'll hitch a ride.' Her voice wobbled with temper. 'And if I were a witch I'd have turned you into a toad weeks ago!'

Any minute now she would slap him, she knew she would. All her emotions were at boiling-point, and somewhere in the muddle was her love for him, the force that was driving her to want to slap him—or kiss him. And her eyes narrowed on a sharp visceral pain as he dragged in a breath through flaring nostrils, his chest expanding against the fine white fabric of his shirt.

Somewhere, during the time he and Cordy had been together, his suit jacket had been discarded along with his tie. And no doubt Cordy could tell her exactly when those garments had been tossed aside. And why. A wave of misery engulfed her, and to relegate it to limbo, where it belonged, she thrust her chin defiantly higher, snorting in temper when he intoned grimly, 'So you would risk who knows what dangers—and I am not talking about blistered feet—simply to defy me?' And he repeated, sounding as if the evidence were impossible to believe, 'You would defy me?'

Oh, what was the use? Cathy thought wrathfully. Scratch a Spaniard and you'd find an autocrat under the skin. Men gave orders and women obeyed. Or else! There was little point in continuing this degrading slanging match, so, carefully tempering her tone, she suggested, 'Well, since you decided to show up at last, you can drive me. To save me getting blisters, of course.'

But she might have been talking to a block of stone for all the expression on his features. And besides, what little light there had been was leaching from the sky, making his response to her suggestion difficult to read. He had gone very still, his body taut, and when he did move, dragging her forward by the wrist, she was taken by surprise.

'Get in.'

Shoved unceremoniously into the passenger seat, Cathy's first thought was that she had won. He was taking her back to Jerez to pack and couldn't be bothered to say all those harsh things he had threatened her with. So why did she want to cry all over again?

Her second thought was that Cordy was missing. He must have dropped her off to spend time with Juan and get to know his mother. Poor Doña Luisa had to be one mightily confused woman!

Cathy stared straight ahead. If Javier chose to keep his own counsel, then so did she. Silence was better than indulging in a slanging match. They were carrying on up the track she had so recently marched down, but that was only because he would find it easier to turn the big car where there was more space, nearer the buildings. So when he pulled up outside the stable block and cut the engine her eyes flashed sideways. But his stony profile revealed absolutely nothing.

'Out!' he snapped, and she had the crazy feeling that he was going to dump her right here, and take himself off again, and leave her here until he decided she'd been punished enough. Or until she grew grey hairs and lost her teeth.

So she stayed exactly where she was, her arms crossed staunchly across her chest. And gave an infuriated gasp when the door was wrenched open at her side, Javier manhandling her, setting her roughly on her feet.

'Tonight there is to be plain talking between us,' he informed her, his long legs planted apart, hands on his narrow hips. 'And tonight I cannot be confined. Wait while I saddle La Llama.'

Cathy trundled after him as he strode to the stables, her mouth compressed. The man had gone crazy! And as he emerged from the tack-room, saddle and bridle over one arm, she said tightly, 'Bawl me out if you have to. But do it now. I don't intend standing here until you get back from your ride.'

'You're coming with me.' The tone of his voice dared her to argue. 'La Llama can carry the two of us easily enough. And as for the bawling out you so richly deserve, it would take me a full year!' The light from the tack-room was behind him, but his voice told her he found her contemptible, and prolonging this discussion—if discussion was the right word—was only prolonging the agony. Riding with him, being that close to him, was quite out of the question. So she would make her apology and, hopefully, that would be the end of that.

'I'm sorry I lied. Sorry I ever pretended to be Juan's mother. I'd like you to try to understand why I did, and how difficult it became to——'

'*Perdición!*' He cut her apology brutally short.

Pig! Maybe she hadn't sounded abject enough? Did his pride demand she grovel at his feet? She clamped her mouth on the impulse to swear right back at him, then it fell open again at his growled, 'I knew you were lying. For a long time I suspected, and then I knew. And, not being stupid, I could work out why. I do not wish to punish you for that, but for running away from me. Just like that.'

He snapped the fingers of his free hand and Cathy muttered, 'There's no need to get all cross and Spanish about it. I wasn't running,' she defended. 'I was beating a tactical retreat. My sister had arrived, wanting her child back—as she is perfectly entitled to do. You could negotiate with her, as I'm sure you already have. You had no further need of me.'

'How do you know my needs?' he demanded, his voice soft and dark with a menace that sent shivers scudding over her flesh, making her own voice thready as she countered,

'From the moment Cordy put in an appearance you made it perfectly obvious. You were furious. You couldn't even bring yourself to speak to me. And as my reason for being here, your reason for wanting to marry me, were both then non-existent, I thought it best to go quietly away.'

'Did I say the wedding would not take place?' he accused in the lordly manner that usually had her secretly aching to kiss him and rumple his hair, but which now had her mouth dropping open. What reason could he possibly have for wanting the marriage to take place now?

But he didn't give her time to voice her tumbling thoughts, striding past her, the tack over his arm, and when she'd gathered herself together she found him leading out the saddled horse, one of the beautiful *cartujanos*, the thoroughbred Arabic-Spanish breed. And she was still in a mental haze as he swung himself into the saddle, hoisted her up in front of him, and put the stallion at a perfectly collected walk across the cobbled surface of the yard.

Still bristling with tension, Cathy had to grit her teeth together to smother a furious demand to be put down. He would do as he pleased. He always had and she supposed he always would. Arguing with him would be a waste of breath. So she tried to use her mental energies in figuring out why, if he had already known of her lies, he had been so angry when Cordy had arrived, explaining who she was, why, as soon as he'd suspected the truth, he hadn't demanded to know the real mother's whereabouts in order to gain her consent to the adoption and sent her, Cathy, packing with a flea in her ear. And found the task beyond her. And gave up thinking altogether when, once on the open *campos*, Javier gave the magnificent stallion his head, and Cathy gave herself up to pure sensation.

The thud of hoofs on the turf was the only sound in the vast, velvet, starlit night, and her body was fire, a burning flame to match the name of the magnificent mount, the conflagration sparked from the enveloping closeness of the Jerezano's lithe strength, his thighs tucked beneath hers, one arm wrapped around her, his hand splayed against the taut swell of her breast, the other lightly holding the reins.

If they could only stay like this forever, she thought dreamily, she and Javier in total physical accord in the warm velvet night, the sleekly muscled animal beneath them carrying them through a softly magical eternity.

Only that wasn't possible, and a nervous tremor rippled through her as Javier reined in the horse and slipped lithely from the saddle. Crunch time began right here, she reasoned, going rigid with inner tension as he lifted his arms to help her down. Out here, in the darkness, miles from anywhere, he could give his temper its head, and she didn't know whether she would be able to survive it, not now when the sensations of the last ten minutes or so had addled her brain and seduced every last one of her senses.

But even though he didn't say a word as he wrapped his arms around her waist and lifted her from the saddle she could sense a change in him. And his grave features seemed touched by sorrow, although, in the glimmering starlight, it was difficult to tell. But his sombre voice reinforced that impression as he said, 'You had promised to marry me, yet you couldn't wait to walk out on me. Am I to understand that with your sister taking a belated interest in Juan, and his future, you saw no reason to stay?'

In a nutshell. Much was missing, but basically that was the truth of it. She had seen him in many moods, some of them quite impossible, but she had never seen him like this. Dolorous was the only word that seemed to fit, and she would rather face his anger than see him like this. And there was a lump in her throat as she whispered, 'Yes.'

'Ah.' A tiny, fraught silence. 'Then the only reason you finally agreed to marry me was to secure Juan's future. That being so, I accept your decision to leave and release you from your promise.' He turned, starlight illuminating the harsh beauty of his profile. 'We will call La Llama from his grazing and return, *señorita*.'

The formality, the finality of his tone, broke her heart all over again. She couldn't let it end like this. And she said quickly, her voice trembling on tears, 'It wasn't the only reason,' and saw his shoulders lift in a small shrug, a tiny nuance of indifference that almost quenched her courage. But, as if the weight of her lies had been too heavy, and borne too long, she told him honestly, 'I agreed because I love you. Because I could hope for no greater happiness than spending the rest of my life with you. And of course Juan was part of it. I love him, too, and for the three of us——'

'*Qué?*'

The deep timbre of his voice, more than the interruption itself, had the words dying away in her throat, and she answered shakily, 'Do I have to repeat myself?'

'Never-endingly, if it is the truth! Is it the truth at last?' He closed the sterile gap between them with one forceful stride, and as she nodded, her heart in her deep violet eyes, his strongs arms enfolded her, dragging her to the virile length of his body. Cathy gasped as his lips claimed hers with savage possession, and the intensity of her love for him had tears streaming down her face when he finally broke away.

'No tears,' he commanded huskily, gentling them out of the way with the balls of his thumbs, his fingers curled around her jaw. 'And no more talk of leaving.' He sank to the ground, pulling her with him. 'We stay here, and we talk here and we order our future, our marriage. But first, *cariño*, we make love. Here, under the stars, we make love.'

Who could disobey such a wickedly exhilarating order, especially when it was put in those rich, purringly black velvet tones? Her mind couldn't quite take in the fact that he still seemed to want her as his wife, despite everything, and she wasn't even going to try to understand it, and gave herself up to sheer wanton pleasure as he began with a slow, lingering thoroughness that gradually, and with sweet inevitability, mounted to untamed passion to make love to her.

And then, in the glorious, floaty aftermath, with his arms wound tightly around her, his sensational mouth covering her face with lingering, tasting kisses, she suddenly remembered and, not really wanting to break this spell, having to push herself into doing it, she asked, her voice disgracefully slurred, 'Where's Cordy?'

'Who?' The movement of his mouth over hers was sinful, and she dragged in a great shuddering breath as his tongue dipped between her lips. And she felt him smile, his mouth curling over hers as he told her, as if it were a thing of no great interest, 'Settling into her hotel in Madrid, I would imagine. Tomorrow she flies back to the States.'

It was too much to take in, and totally unlikely, and she couldn't concentrate, because he had edged himself upon one elbow and his hand was drifting over her nakedness, demonstrating his mastery of everything sensual, and it was a struggle to absorb his words as he said indifferently, 'After an initial couple of hours alone with my lawyers this morning your sister and I spent another three agreeing the terms of a settlement which was duly, and without duress, signed by her. It ensures her a handsome income for life, and the right to see her son whenever she wishes—and I somehow don't think she'll wish very often—in return for her consent to his eventual legal adoption by you, and by me. I then drove her to the airport and waited until she boarded an internal flight to Madrid.'

So that was where he had been! And Cordy had sold her son for a pot of gold. But that didn't matter, did it? She and Javier would give him all the love and emotional security he needed. More than he needed. And she really was in heaven, and his hand was lingering on the satin softness of her inner thigh. Greedily, she turned to him, but he smiled in the darkness.

'Such a willing wanton, *amor mío*! However, there is one thing I would like to know before I gladly satisfy your delightful eagerness.' He gathered her to him, the evidence of his ability to do just that making her cry out deliriously, bringing his mouth down on hers with a hard, swift, responsive kiss. 'Why didn't you tell me who you were when I first found you and Juan? Did you think I was incapable of listening, of sorting everything out for the benefit of all? Did you think me evil? And even if you did, couldn't you bring yourself to trust me when you got to know me better?' His voice was raw around the edges and she smoothed her fingers over the sleek warmth of his shoulders, tracing the forceful line of his collarbone as he asked, 'Can you understand how, when I was as sure as I could be that my suspicions were right, that you must have a sister—Cordelia—your lack of trust in my good intentions both hurt and angered me?'

'Oh, Javier,' she breathed tremulously, understanding now those bouts of simmering rage which, at the time, she had put down to her refusal to give a definite answer to his proposal. Curling herself snugly into his body, she told him how she'd been afraid that if he knew the truth he would have taken the baby she loved from her. How, having lied or, at best, omitted to tell the truth, she found herself enmeshed by the web of deceit and put even under more constraint when she found herself falling in love with him.

'I'd been meaning to tell you everything and let you decide whether or not you still wanted to marry me. And then Cordy appeared and you were so angry——'

'But not with you, *querida*.' He cradled her tightly. 'With her. I had already guessed you weren't the flighty, second-rate-model girl I'd seen with Francisco. But I knew you had to be related. There was this likeness, you see. At first I was merely puzzled. You were far more beautiful than I remembered and much more loving and maternal than my enquiries into the character of the woman who had borne my brother's child had led me to expect. I set out to find my nephew and his mother full of misgivings, due to what I'd heard. And maybe I was harsh, or too outspoken in my intention to see that Juan was properly cared for, and that was why you lied by omission. Completely understandable.' His hands stroked her back. 'You are not cold?'

She shook her head, loving him. The night air was like warm silk. He had actually said she was more beautiful than her sister! Could it possibly be true? She would ask him! But he was saying, 'And I lied to you, Cathy *mia*. When I first brought you here I told you that Madre had not yet suficiently come to terms with

Francisco's death to see you and the child. In reality, of course, she was anxious to meet you both. I had to be stern to make her stay away! But I needed to observe you closely. You didn't fit in with what I'd come to expect. You were devoted to the baby, a soft and generously loving woman. Not at all the creature of dubious moral and avaricious selfishness I had been led to expect. The increased loveliness, those delightful curves, I put down to recent motherhood. But the rest——'

'And so you decided to test me,' Cathy put in gently, not minding, because she understood why he had done it. 'When we met that day, out here on the *campos*, and you tried to seduce me, you were trying to prove I had few morals.'

'*Dios*!' He gave a short bark of laughter. 'I tried to make love to you because I wanted to. I couldn't help myself. You were exquisite; I couldn't keep my hands off you. And later I had the idea of marrying you. I amazed myself. And, to square me with myself, I told you and me both that it would be a marriage in name only, simply for the sake of making my care of Francisco's child more straightforward in the future. And later still, even as my suspicions as to your true identity grew stronger, I faced the fact that I wanted you for my wife, my lover, the mother of my children. And when you agreed I brought you here. I knew, if I gave you the time, and the opportunity, you would tell me the truth yourself. And you started to. You told me about your first love, and all my suspicions were confirmed. Your sister would have had difficulty in picking one man out from the the rest. And you said, or implied, that there had been only the one. So where did my brother come into it? And so we come full circle.' He moved to cover her body gently with his, and she lifted her hips enticingly. And the lack of the need for any enticement at all was shown in the growly tone of his voice against her throat. 'Cordelia walked in, uninvited and unwanted, just as you were about to make your confession. And I was angry enough to slay her on the spot, because I'd had a confession of my own to make.'

'And that was?' she prompted, breathless because of the tiny kisses he was dancing down her throat, closer and ever closer to the aching globes of her full breasts.

'*Te quiero muchisimo, querida.* I think I fell in love with you right here, out on the *campos*. And that is why I brought you here tonight. To end it all where it had first begun for me.'

'Only there is no end, is there?' she stated, rejoicing in his love, the strength of her feelings for him, and he whispered, his voice thick with passion,

'No end to our love or our loving. Let me show you, *amor mío*.'

And as the dawn painted rosy circles across the sky, they walked back to the *finca*, hand in hand, La Llama following, sometimes thrusting a helpful nose against Cathy's back, sometimes against Javier's, as if to say he had been patient long enough and now wanted his stable and a good breakfast.

'Tell me why you refused to say a single word to me after Cordy arrived,' Cathy asked very casually. She didn't mind if he told her that, at that moment, he had wanted to slay her, too. She was secure in his love now, happier than she had ever believed possible, but he confounded her again, slipping a loving arm around her waist, his voice threaded with reminiscent amusement.

'I didn't have the time to say all I had to say to you. So I decided to get right on with sorting your sister out, seeing my lawyer and making an offer she couldn't refuse. Only then, when that was completed, could I come to you and tell you I loved you. But when I arrived to take the unsuspecting Cordy to meet with my lawyers, you were on the point of departure. There was no time then to do other than threaten you with hell-fire unless you stayed exactly where you were until I returned with everything under control. And when I found you attempting to hitch-hike to town, in order to leave me, my desolation was reinforced. If only I had known then what I know now. . .'

His arm tightened around her, his voice failing, as if his heart was too full to allow further speech, and she snuggled closer to his side, and consoled, *'Te quiero, amado.'*

Dipping his head briefly to touch her lips with his, he smiled. 'Your accent is excruciating! But we have all the time in the world to remedy that. I shall teach you my language, which will become your language. And, to reward you, we will visit England from time to time. You will not be homesick,' he stated, at his most lordly as he handed La Llama over to one of the grooms who came hurrying over the cobbles of the stable-yard at the sound of their approach, the lad's eyes commendably lowered, at odds with his mirthfully twitching lips as he registered the untidy state of their clothing.

'Having lived here in Andalusia, particularly in Jerez, no one could possibly be homesick for anywhere else in the world,' he continued, his grey eyes dancing as he led her by the hand through the arch leading to the courtyard. 'However, I shall humour you in your possible need to visit the country of your birth, as in all else.'

And standing here, with him, with the dew on the roses, the fragrant lilies, with the early mist throwing a gauzy veil across the rising sun, she could think of no better place to be.

But she looked deep into his serene grey eyes, her own suddenly serious as she asked, 'And Juan. . .? I will give you children—but will he still have a place in your heart when you have sons of your own?'

'Always!' he caught her roughly to his power-packed body, holding her against his heart. 'However many babies you give me, however deeply I love them, Juan will always have a special place in my affections. Without him, we would never have met and I would never have known what it is to love one woman to the exclusion of all else, to know that I am capable of a deep and abiding passion that is as much deeper than the mere lusts of the flesh as the ocean is deeper than a raindrop. And now——' he set her a little away from him, tilting her chin with his hand, smiling into her eyes '—it is time for breakfast. Paquita shall bring it out here to us. And then a long, leisurely bath and a much earlier than usual siesta. We had a busy night. You agree?'

She tilted her head to one side, her eyes luxuriated in the sensual line of his mouth, and laughter bubbled inside her as she countered, 'Would a dutiful Spanish wife ever dare to disagree?' Her eyes glinted wickedly. 'You see how happy I am to get into training? And you do mean together, don't you? The leisurely bath and the long siesta?'

'Together. Always.'

And the words of her Jerezano contained all the promise and passion she could ever need, or handle.

Welcome to Europe

ANDALUSIA

Whatever you're searching for, you'll find it in Andalusia. There are historical cities, little villages, high mountains and golden beaches where you can lie and listen to the gentle lapping of the waves on the shore. Exploring the area, you'll come across orange and palm trees, and olive trees distinctively set out in neat rows. Add to this the sunshine Spain is well known for, and you've the perfect setting for love. And for the final touch of romance, just imagine a Spaniard serenading his lover with the lilting music of a guitar. . .

THE ROMANTIC PAST

The history of Andalusia is long and colourful. **Neanderthal man** could be found in the area some 50,000 years ago, and the **Iberians** are thought to have arrived around 7000 BC. In 711 the **Moors** arrived, and cities such as Málaga and Seville prospered. For a while Andalusia's wealth, art and architecture were superior to those anywhere else in Europe.

The year of 1212 is said to be as important in Spanish history as the year 1066 is in British history. This was the year of the **Battle of Navas de Tolosa**, when an army of Christians from the north of Spain aimed to attack the very heart of Andalusia and succeeded in winning the Battle of the Reconquest over the Muslims. The leader of the march apparently vowed that he would not touch a woman until he won — which no doubt gave him an extra incentive!

The Andalusian town of **Cádiz** claims to be the oldest city in Western Europe. Its inhabitants claim it was founded by Hercules. Whether this is true or not, Cádiz has certainly had some famous visitors. Julius Caesar took control of it for a while, and Francis Drake also came here.

Although Spain is known for being warm and sunny it has some fierce winds. Cádiz in Andalusia is sometimes visited by a strange wind called the *solano*. Legend goes that this wind used to have a very strange effect on the female inhabitants of the town. Apparently in the old days they would gather on the beach, strip off their clothes and then jump in the sea for relief, with the local cavalry regiment standing guard. Men planning to visit the town may be disappointed to find that this custom no longer takes place.

Andalusia's most famous son is probably **Picasso**, who was born in Málaga. You might have thought the beautiful Andalusian scenery might have tempted him to put pen to paper, but he claims the first thing he ever drew was a *churros*, a rather unappetising-sounding Spanish food which consists of a wad of greasy fried dough.

Attractive **Seville** has inspired many poets and composers. Bizet's Carmen is supposed to have rolled her cigarettes in the Royal Tobacco Factory, while Seville is also said to have been the birthplace of Don Juan, who became Mozart's *Don Giovanni*, and the setting for *The Marriage of Figaro*.

THE ROMANTIC PRESENT — pastimes for lovers. . .

The region of Andalusia offers many delights to explore, and what better place to start than **Seville**, Andalusia's capital? This is Spain's fourth largest city, and is especially attractive in spring, when the air is full of the scent of flowers.

One building you won't be able to miss in Seville in the **Cathedral of Santa María**. It is the third largest Christian church in the world, after St Peter's in Rome and St Paul's in London, and it took one hundred years to build. Its bell-tower, **La Giralda**, is particularly famous, and can be seen from anywhere in the city. To get to the top and enjoy a superb view you have to go up a series of ramps. These were built to be wide enough for Fernando II to ride his horse up for the view, but unfortunately these days you'll have to walk!

The **Archaeological Museum** in Seville is well worth a visit, as is the eighteenth-century **tobacco factory**, which is famous for being the setting for Bizet's opera *Carmen*.

After you've explored the main buildings in Seville you might like to visit the area of **Barrio Santa Cruz** to discover another side to the city. If it's romance you're looking for you'll be hard pressed to find a better spot—there are whitewashed houses in tiny narrowed streets, and flowers adorn the patios. You may even be lucky enough to witness one of the young men in the district serenading his sweetheart with a guitar.

The weather in Seville is usually so pleasant that you'll probably want to spend a lot of time in the fresh air, and there are few better places than the beautiful **María Luisa park**. Here you can stroll among palm and orange trees, or relax with only the gentle sound of splashing water from a fountain to disturb you.

There's enough to keep you occupied in Seville for weeks, but Andalusia has many other delights to offer, so if you're lucky enough to have a car you may like to visit other towns or villages. **Cádiz**, to the south of Seville, is well worth a visit, especially if you're interested in history. Sights worth seeing include the charming eighteenth-century cathedral and the **Museum of Fine Arts and Archaeology**. Or take a wander round the **Plaza Topete**, a bustling and colourful market area.

After reading this Euromance you may want to visit the place where much of it is set—**Jerez de la Frontera**. If you like sherry you'll probably want to visit one of the *bodegas*, where you will be shown round the huge caverns and have the opportunity to taste various blends. But will you resist being able to buy a few bottles to take back home with you?

Sightseeing is fascinating, but there are times when all you really want to do on holiday is relax on a sun-drenched beach—and, with the **Costa Del Sol** close at hand, you have the perfect opportunity to spend a few days enjoying the sun, sand and *sangria* in resorts such as Marbella, Fuengirola or Torremolinos.

These resorts aren't the place to come if you want to get away from it all, though—or if you want to feel you're really in Spain. In fact there are so many tourists that one shop in Fuengirola has a sign saying '*Se habla Español*'—Spanish spoken here!

At the end of the day—whether you've been busy sightseeing or lazing on a beach—there's nothing better than enjoying some typically Spanish food. You might choose to start your meal with **gazpacho**, a delicious cold tomato, cucumber and onion soup. For the main course you might want to choose fish. Particularly recommended are **red bream, shellfish** and **molluscs, grilled sardines** and **fried baby anchovies**. An Andalusian speciality if you're feeling brave is **rabo de toro**—bull's tail cooked with sauce.

Rather than having a full meal at a restaurant, you might like to eat at a **tapas bar**. Here you'll find plates of titbits, from omelette to shellfish to vegetables in sauces. You just point to what you'd like and muck in—along with some beer or wine, of course.

And talking of drink, if you're on holiday in Andalusia you're likely to want to try some **sherry**. There are several varieties—*manzanilla* is very dry, *fino* is dry and light, *amontillado* is a little sweeter and richer, and *oloroso* is a very sweet dessert sherry.

If you're not a sherry fan, there's still plenty of drinks to choose from. Spanish wine is both good and inexpensive, and beer is very popular. And after relaxing on the beach, sharing a mug of *sangria* with your partner is the perfect way to end the day. Made of red wine, brandy, mineral water and orange and lemon, it's very refreshing — but can also be quite potent!

After eating and drinking, it's time to go out for the evening. If you'd like to see a display of **flamenco dancing**, Andalusia is the ideal place to do so, as flamenco dancing actually began here in the eighteenth century. If you want to see an authentic display, rather than one of the more obvious displays put on for the tourists, try asking in bars in Seville, or, if you're lucky enough to come across one, attending a festival in an Andalusian village.

Before you go home, you'll probably want some souvenirs to remind you of your holiday. Good buys include **leather** shoes or bags, especially from Córdoba, bottles of **sherry** and **ceramic plates** and **pottery**. Just don't forget to leave enough room in your suitcase to pack them all!

DID YOU KNOW THAT. . .?

* Andalusia has about one-fifth of Spain's population and its biggest tourist industry.

* the Spanish currency is the **peseta**.

* every city in Andalusia except for Huelva and Jaen has had an American or Spanish **car** named after it.

* in Spanish history there are characters with names such as **Wilfred the Hairy** and **Alfonso the Slobberer**,

while there are villages whose names can be translated to mean **Chaos, Onion,** and the **New Village of the Ill-tempered!**

* the way to say 'I love you' in Spain is '*Te quiero*'.

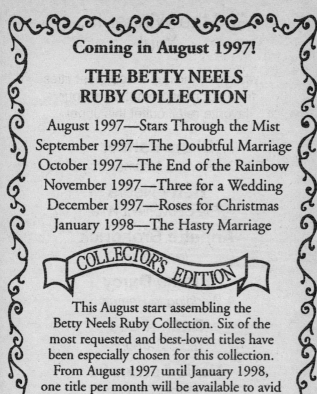

Coming in August 1997!

THE BETTY NEELS RUBY COLLECTION

August 1997—Stars Through the Mist
September 1997—The Doubtful Marriage
October 1997—The End of the Rainbow
November 1997—Three for a Wedding
December 1997—Roses for Christmas
January 1998—The Hasty Marriage

COLLECTOR'S EDITION

This August start assembling the
Betty Neels Ruby Collection. Six of the
most requested and best-loved titles have
been especially chosen for this collection.
From August 1997 until January 1998,
one title per month will be available to avid
fans. Spot the collection by the lush ruby red
cover with the gold Collector's Edition banner
and your favorite author's name—Betty Neels!

Available in August at your favorite retail outlet.

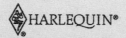

HARLEQUIN®

And the Winner Is...
You!

...when you pick up these great titles
from our new promotion at your
favorite retail outlet this June!

Diana Palmer
The Case of the Mesmerizing Boss

Betty Neels
The Convenient Wife

Annette Broadrick
Irresistible

Emma Darcy
A Wedding to Remember

Rachel Lee
Lost Warriors

Marie Ferrarella
Father Goose

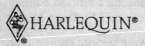 

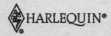 

HARLEQUIN PRESENTS®

Coming soon...

June 1997—Long Night's Loving (#1887)

by Anne Mather

New York Times bestselling author,
with over 60 million books in print

"Pleasure for her readers."   —*Romantic Times*

and

July 1997—A Haunting Obsession (#1893)

by Miranda Lee

one of Presents' brightest stars,
with over 10 million books sold worldwide

"Superb storytelling."   —*Romantic Times*

Top author treats from Harlequin Presents.
Make this summer the hottest ever!

FORTUNE COOKIE

Breathtaking romance is predicted in your future with Harlequin's newest collection: Fortune Cookie.

Three of your favorite Harlequin authors, Janice Kaiser, Margaret St. George and M.J. Rodgers will regale you with the romantic adventures of three heroines who are promised fame, fortune, danger and intrigue when they crack open their fortune cookies on a fateful night at a Chinese restaurant.

Join in the adventure with your own personalized fortune, inserted in every book!

Don't miss this exciting new collection!

Available in September wherever Harlequin books are sold.

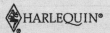

HARLEQUIN®

Look us up on-line at: http://www.romance.net   FCOOKIE

Don't miss these Harlequin favorites by some of our most popular authors! And now you can receive a discount by ordering two or more titles!

HT#25700	HOLDING OUT FOR A HERO		
	by Vicki Lewis Thompson	$3.50 U.S. ☐	/$3.99 CAN.☐
HT#25699	WICKED WAYS		
	by Kate Hoffmann	$3.50 U.S. ☐	/$3.99 CAN.☐
HP#11845	RELATIVE SINS		
	by Anne Mather	$3.50 U.S. ☐	/$3.99 CAN.☐
HP#11849	A KISS TO REMEMBER		
	by Miranda Lee	$3.50 U.S. ☐	/$3.99 CAN.☐
HR#03359	FAITH, HOPE AND MARRIAGE		
	by Emma Goldrick	$2.99 U.S. ☐	/$3.50 CAN.☐
HR#03433	TEMPORARY HUSBAND		
	by Day Leclaire	$3.25 U.S. ☐	/$3.75 CAN.☐
HS#70679	QUEEN OF THE DIXIE DRIVE-IN		
	by Peg Sutherland	$3.99 U.S. ☐	/$4.50 CAN.☐
HS#70712	SUGAR BABY		
	by Karen Young	$3.99 U.S. ☐	/$4.50 CAN.☐
HI#22319	BREATHLESS		
	by Carly Bishop	$3.50 U.S. ☐	/$3.99 CAN.☐
HI#22335	BEAUTY VS. THE BEAST		
	by M.J. Rodgers	$3.50 U.S. ☐	/$3.99 CAN.☐
AR#16577	BRIDE OF THE BADLANDS		
	by Jule McBride	$3.50 U.S. ☐	/$3.99 CAN.☐
AR#16656	RED-HOT RANCHMAN		
	by Victoria Pade	$3.75 U.S. ☐	/$4.25 CAN.☐
HH#28868	THE SAXON		
	by Margaret Moore	$4.50 U.S. ☐	/$4.99 CAN.☐
HH#28893	UNICORN VENGEANCE		
	by Claire Delacroix	$4.50 U.S. ☐	/$4.99 CAN.☐

(limited quantities available on certain titles)

	TOTAL AMOUNT	$ _____
DEDUCT:	10% DISCOUNT FOR 2+ BOOKS	$ _____
	POSTAGE & HANDLING	$ _____
	($1.00 for one book, 50¢ for each additional)	
	APPLICABLE TAXES*	$ _____
	TOTAL PAYABLE	$ _____

(check or money order—please do not send cash)

To order, complete this form, along with a check or money order for the total above, payable to Harlequin Books, to: **In the U.S.:** 3010 Walden Avenue, P.O. Box 9047, Buffalo, NY 14269-9047; **In Canada:** P.O. Box 613, Fort Erie, Ontario, L2A 5X3.

Name: _____

Address: _____ City: _____

State/Prov.: _____ Zip/Postal Code: _____

*New York residents remit applicable sales taxes.
Canadian residents remit applicable GST and provincial taxes.

Look us up on-line at: http://www.romance.net

HBKJS97

Let's Celebrate!

LOVE & LAUGHTER™

invites you to
the party of the season!

Grab your popcorn and be prepared to laugh as we celebrate with **LOVE & LAUGHTER**.

Harlequin's newest series is going Hollywood!

Let us make you laugh with three months of terrific books, authors and romance, plus a chance to win a FREE 15-copy video collection of the best romantic comedies ever made.

For more details look in the back pages of any Love & Laughter title, from July to September, at your favorite retail outlet.

Don't forget the popcorn!

Available wherever
Harlequin books are sold.

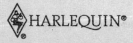

Look us up on-line at: http://www.romance.net

LLCELEB